PENGUIN BOOKS
HALF A RUPEE

Gulzar is one of India's most respected scriptwriters and film directors, and has been one of the most popular lyricists in mainstream Hindi cinema for over five decades. One of the country's leading poets, he has published a number of poetry anthologies and collections of short stories. He is also regarded as one of India's finest writers for children.

Apart from many Filmfare and National Awards for his films and lyrics—and an Oscar and Grammy for the song *Jai ho*—Gulzar has received the Sahitya Akademi Award in 2002 and the Padma Bhushan in 2004. He lives and works in Mumbai.

Sunjoy Shekhar was born in Sahibganj, a small, sleepy town in Jharkhand on the banks of the river Ganga. He started work as an editor with a Delhi-based publishing house before moving on to writing dramas for television. He has more than 10,000 hours of story-writing credits across a host of television channels in India and Indonesia. He has also translated Gulzar's *100 Lyrics*.

W0232848

BY THE SAME AUTHOR

Selected Poems, translated by Pavan K. Varma
100 Lyrics, translated by Sunjoy Shekhar
Neglected Poems, translated by Pavan K. Varma
Yudhishtar and Draupadi, translation of a work by
Pavan K. Varma

Half a Rupee
Stories

GULZAR

Translated by
SUNJOY SHEKHAR

PENGUIN BOOKS

An imprint of Penguin Random House

PENGUIN BOOKS

USA | Canada | UK | Ireland | Australia
New Zealand | India | South Africa | China | Singapore

Penguin Books is part of the Penguin Random House group of companies
whose addresses can be found at global.penguinrandomhouse.com

Published by Penguin Random House India Pvt. Ltd
4th Floor, Capital Tower 1, MG Road,
Gurugram 122 002, Haryana, India

First published by Penguin Books India 2013

12 11 10 9 8 7 6

ISBN 9780143068792

Typeset in Palatino by InoSoft Systems, Noida
Printed at Manipal Technologies Limited, India

www.penguin.co.in

MIX
Paper | Supporting
responsible forestry
FSC® C043100

for

SALIM ARIF AND LUBNA SALIM

Contents

IV

V

VI

VII

VIII

Foreword

I wish I didn't have to write a Foreword to my stories. I have nothing to explain about a story, if it doesn't explain itself.

Of course there are various subjects on which I have written. But then life is not lived in a monotone. You pass through a variety of phases, both personally and socially. You meet a galaxy of people in the orbit of your days and nights. I have touched on a few.

Don't be surprised if you find yourself reading about some well-known names. Some of these stories are biographical in a way. There are many who have shared some emotional experiences with me, and I am sharing them with others.

Humra Quraishi is one person I would like to mention in particular. We shared a lot of Kashmir though neither of us is from there.

Some of these stories were translated by Devina Dutt earlier and published in *Indian Literature*, the journal of the Sahitya Akademi. But all the stories have been translated anew by Sunjoy Shekhar, to give them uniformity of style and expression. Sunjoy is an inimitable writer and an intimate friend; he has a way with words.

Last—but foremost—is Udayan Mitra: he has given a shine to my work. I agreed to publish this collection on one condition: that he would edit my book. He has done all my earlier books too. And I will come back again, only if he has the time to edit my work. Thank you, Udayan.

Mumbai   Gulzar
December 2012

Introduction

When I was growing up on the cobbled streets of small-town Bihar, night always appeared to fall early. Before the streets could echo with the sounds of conch shells and the ululation of mothers and aunts performing their pujas, we children would be dragged by the scruff of our dusty, mangy collars by elder sisters to be scrubbed clean and placed before piles of waiting homework—before they could stoke the coal in the evening chullahs. In the spiralling smoke of those chullahs you could almost see our prayers rising to petition the Old Man in the sky. All the kids, praying in unison, asking for just one thing—a power cut, the longer the better. And when the street would suddenly plunge into darkness, hundreds of tiny feet would break free, leap out of houses, milling around a man we knew only as Makoria Mamu. He had only half a tongue.

The other half he claimed his stepmother had cut off. God knows whose mamu he was, or why he was called Makoria—'spidery'—but he sure had a web of stories to brighten our darkest nights. We would huddle around him in rapt attention as he spun his narratives—with only half his tongue—around people we knew, around things that happened in our real lives, parables masquerading as real, tangible adventures. At the end of his stories, he would demand a chapatti from each one of us. There was hardly a household in the mohalla that did not make one extra chapatti for Makoria Mamu. We never saw him before dark, and I never saw him ever again when I swapped my small town for big-city India.

It is believed that a community, a society, a nation is as strong and healthy as the stories they tell themselves. In this collection of twenty-five stories—with a cast of characters to rival the residents of a Naipaulian Miguel Street—I can smell my Makoria Mamu.

Gulzar saab has always told stories in his songs. But when he writes short stories, he peppers them with the verve of a Bhagwati Charan Varma, the compassion of a Mahadevi Varma; he morphs these stories into songs of a kind that make these characters greater than the sum of their sufferings. The powerful alchemy of his storytelling transforms the *atthanni*—the half a rupee coin—into a rupaiya.

These stories can make your heart grow larger. A story sprouts wherever the men and women who populate this book appear—be it a far-flung desert outpost or the storage godown of a film studio. The characters in this book are born into their own stories, but it is only when Gulzar, the writer, is born out of these stories that he finds shelter: 'tum hee se janmoon toh shayad panah miley'.

The magic of storytelling is derived from our ability to summon up all our thoughts about who we are and where we are going, by our ability to take lives that are lived in halves and make them whole. A good storyteller is the conscience-keeper of a nation.

And Gulzar saab is a good storyteller.

I had a blast translating these stories and I just hope that I was able to capture the magic of Gulzar saab's originals in my translations. If I have succeeded even in a small measure, the credit must go to Udayan Mitra, an editor every writer should pray for, and to my wife of twenty years, Geeta. I would like to dedicate my translations to my Subhash Mamu, and to my daughter Gauraa in the hope that she can see a world that she could not read about in the original Urdu. I also need to thank Manoj Punjabi, without whose magnanimity I would not have found the time to finish this book.

Jakarta   Sunjoy Shekhar
December 2012

I

Walk through the pages of a book and
You'll find characters, like old friends
In the corridors of time—

Kuldip Nayyar and Pir Sahib

I remember it was a Friday, the evening of 14 August 1998. Kuldip Nayyar and I were driving towards the Wagah border.

Nayyar Sahib had been doing this without fail for quite some time. Every year on 14 August he would land up at the Wagah border with a few scholars, poets, artists and littérateurs. During the change of guards, when the flags of the two nations are lowered, he and his friends would rend the air with slogans of Indo–Pak friendship. They would light lamps at the border post and keep up their candlelight vigil till the clocks struck the turn of a new day. This was how he and his friends celebrated the two Independence Days of a pair of twins born a day apart.

It was a long straight road to Wagah. The evening was gathering darkness and Nayyar Sahib was saying, 'If the road keeps going straight ahead like this and there are no roadblocks, no checkposts, no hindrances or obstructions of any kind—and if I go visit Pakistan for a little while, what harm will I cause to that country, what will I have pillaged? Not that there is a dearth of pillagers and plunderers in that country or ours. No one needs to raid our countries from the outside.'

A hush fell over us. After a long pause Nayyar Sahib said, 'After all, that country too is my home. A large part of me still lives on that side of the border.'

He must have seen some sort of question floating in my eyes, for he elaborated further: 'My school is over there—my madrasa. My teacher, Master Dinanath, and my maulvi, Ismail. My alphabet primer, my school bags, they still are across the border. My roots still remain on the other side. I have only cut loose the branches and tugged them along with me.'

Nayyar Sahib's voice was increasingly tinged with veneration for what was once his home. That day, Sialkot took over his thoughts often. 'All of us, uncles and aunts—father's elder brother, younger brother, his brother-in-law—we all had our houses next to each other, in the same lane. Right in front of our house was a large space. An open space. Not a single brick wall to mark a boundary. Not a single peg hammered in the ground to delineate one house from another. Enough space for everybody. No need to squabble over it. Right across this open space was a big leafy pipal tree. It was closer to our house than any of my uncles'. And right under the tree's canopy, near the foot of its trunk was a grave. It was unmarked. We had no idea whose bones lay under the raised mound of mud, but Ma often said that it was the holy Pir Baba's grave, and that was how it was known.

'Ma would anoint the trunk of the pipal with sindoor and light a diya, an earthen lamp, on the grave. She would dip her finger in the small pot of sindoor and smear it on the pipal but would wipe the rich vermillion smeared on her finger clean against the exposed bricks of the grave. She would light the diya, do the aarti of the pipal but would place the lit diya in the crumbling alcove of the tombstone. When an offering was made to the pipal, an offering would be made to the Pir Sahib as well. If things had upset her at home, she would go and sit leaning against the trunk of the pipal and talk for hours on end to Pir Sahib. At times she would even cry her heart out. Thus unburdened, she would glide back to the house, and bring the Pir Sahib along too. Poor Pir Sahib! He knew of no peace even in his grave. Ma would summon him from his rest all the time.

'I remember during our school examinations, Ma would say, "Bow your head before Pir Sahib, seek his blessing before you go." Whether it was examinations or festivals, moments of celebration or mourning, there was no happiness big enough and no sadness small enough not to involve Pir Sahab. There was no respite for him.'

Lapsing into colloquial Punjabi, Nayyar Sahib said, 'If an important question needed to be answered, some decision needed to be made, it was Pir Sahib's advice that Ma sought. We never got any answers from Pir Sahib, but Ma would get signs from him. At times, Ma would say that Pir Sahib came in her dreams and told her what to do.'

We had reached Wagah. The sun was about to set. The flags of both the countries were lowered in a ritualistic retreat ceremony. There were a few people on the Pakistan side and a handful on ours. Film star Raj Babbar had joined us. The celebrated lawyer and human rights activist Asma Jahangir was supposed to be on the other side, but eventually she did not turn up; she was not allowed to by her government. At the stroke of midnight we all lit candles at the border. We took a few pictures and rent the air thick with Indo–Pak friendship slogans. And with a lump in our a-little-parched-a-little-choked throats, we returned.

The next day we were on the way to Delhi. But I wanted to trek back to Sialkot. So I picked up the threads of our old conversation. 'Nayyar Sahib, your mother saw the Pir Sahib in her dreams. Did you ever ask her what the Pir Sahib looked like, how he appeared to be?'

Nayyar Sahib was in a different mood now. A smile appeared on his lips and he said, 'I started off as an investigative journalist. It was in my nature to ask. And ask I did. And to tell you the truth, I found Pir Sahib to be exactly the way Ma told me.'

'Found him . . . meaning . . . you . . . you . . . met him?'

He kept smiling. And said, 'In 1975 when Indira Gandhi declared an Emergency, I was amongst the political leaders and intellectuals she threw behind bars. That day too was a Friday—I remember it vividly. 24 July

1975. They kept me in Tihar Jail. The jailer told me that my incarceration was only momentary and that I would be released soon. When I asked him who gave the orders, all he said was a single word: "Madam." But when a few days passed without any sign of release I requested the jailer if he could fetch me my books and journals. He was a gentleman, the jailer. Not only did he get me what I had asked for, he made sure that I was provided with a table and a table lamp.

'The period of my incarceration began to lengthen at an arduously slow pace. And then one day when I lost hope, I asked him when I would be released.'

I kept quiet. Nayyar Sahib too just kept looking at me in silence. We were now sitting in the airport lounge in Amritsar. Suddenly, the penny dropped: 'Him? You asked him? Whom?'

He was perhaps waiting for me to explicitly raise this question and said, 'Pir Sahib, who else?'

'Oh!'

'He came to me in my dreams. Dressed in flowing green robes with a long white beard. That's how Ma had described him and that's how I saw him. I do not remember if his head was covered . . .'

'What did he say?'

'He said that I would be a free man by Thursday.'

'Did he say anything else?'

'Yes . . . he said, "I am feeling too cold, beta. Give your shawl to me, son."' And Nayyar Sahib laughed.

'So, you were released . . . I mean were you released by Thursday?'

'No. Come Thursday, I became very restless. Not because I was still cooped up in the jail . . . but for Pir Sahib . . . I don't know why but I wanted his promise to come true . . . perhaps I wanted to believe in him . . . I don't know. As was my habit, I kept working late into the night and got up late the next day. It was on Friday morning that the jailer came to me with my release orders. 11 September 1975. A little surprised, I looked at him and asked, "When did these orders come?"

'"The release orders arrived last night only. But by the time I came on duty it was quite late. You were at your desk, working, and you had given us strict instructions not to disturb you."

'I looked at him, my voice reinforced by faith, and reiterated, "Yesterday! You mean the release orders arrived on Thursday night?"

'The jailer hesitated for a moment and then looked at me, "Yes sir! . . . You already knew about it?"

'And I happily told him, "Yes, I had prior information!"'

There was more to this incident. Nayyar Sahib said that when his mother got to know about it, she told him, 'Son, you must make a pilgrimage to his tomb in Sialkot. You must offer him the shawl. He must be really feeling cold.'

'Tears had welled up in Ma's eyes,' Nayyar Sahib recounted. 'But I was not able to go to Sialkot immediately thereafter. Those days it was difficult to acquire a visa to visit Sialkot. But when Ma passed away in 1990 I felt obligated to go. When I reached Sialkot I found the place where we once lived had become totally different. It was unrecognizable. The huge open space in front of our house was divided up into small shops. The whole place had taken the shape of a market. And the grave was nowhere to be found. I asked almost everybody I met but no one knew about the grave, no one remembered it. It did not exist in their memories. I somehow approximated the place where the giant pipal had once stood. There was no sign of the tree or the grave.

'A shop now stood there instead. I kept visiting the shopkeeper every day. And he stayed true to his refrain that he had not seen any grave, did not know about one. Then when I was about to return I bumped into the same shopkeeper, this time outside the market area. And he accosted me, saying, "Whose grave was it? The grave that you were looking for?"

'I told him it was the grave of a Pir. My mother had great faith in him.

'The man became a little uneasy at this. He hemmed and hawed but finally with great reluctance confessed, "Yes, there certainly was a grave here, adjacent to our shop. We were refugees. In those days we lived in the shop only. There hardly was any space. It was too confined. And then we encroached upon the grave. In order to live, we had to steal the space of a grave from the dead."

'I came back. And then one day I went to the dargah of Nizamuddin Auliya and the shawl that I had taken with me to Sialkot, I offered at the tomb.'

'Did he come in your dreams ever again?'

'No! How I wished he had! Many a times in my hours of darkness, in my times of trouble, I wished he would come to me in my dreams. I wished I could ask him a few things. How I longed for his advice, his answers. But he never did. Perhaps he left this earth along with Ma. Finally, he had got his respite. Finally, he had found salvation.'

Sahir and Jaadu

A ll this happened before they hoisted Sahir's mortal remains up on their shoulders and took him out on his last journey. It was Jaadu who told me the story.

Jaadu and Sahir: Sahir, as in Sahir Ludhianvi and Jaadu, as in Javed Akhtar.

Their relationship was not your run-of-the-mill kind. The bonds that held them together were quite unique.

Jaadu is Javed Akhtar's nickname. Magnanimous to a fault, his inclination runs towards everything poetic. Poetry flows in his veins. And why shouldn't it—he comes from an illustrious lineage of poets: Jaan Nisar Akhtar for a father, and Majaz for a maternal uncle. If that wasn't enough, he later got Kaifi Azmi for a father-in-law.

But Jaadu could never bring himself to respect his father. An unrelenting anger against his father would

be forever seething inside him. As long as his mother
was alive, he bore with his father. But after her death, he
began to find his father insufferable. Often, at the slightest
provocation, he would barge out of his house and make
a beeline for Sahir's. Just one look at his face and Sahir
would know that father and son had had another of
their fracas. But he would never ever let Jaadu get even
a whiff of his suspicion. Heaven forbid if he would even
hint at it: Jaadu's nostrils would first flare, then he would
explode in anger, and finally, spent, disintegrate into
tears. Sahir did not relish the prospect of being witness
to any of these demonstrations. Sahir would just let Jaadu
be, give him some space, and, after a brief interval, call
out to him, 'Jaadu! Come . . . grab some grub!' And while
munching on his food, Jaadu would crunch out his anger
and pour his heart out to Sahir. He would spend the entire
day at Sahir's house, and tell him everything: Father did
this . . . Father did that . . . The day would end but not
Jaadu's list of grievances against his father.

But Sahir would not be able to indulge him like this
every time. Some days, he would interrupt Jaadu's litany
of complaints against his father with a warning, 'Akhtar's
coming over for lunch!' Jaadu would arch his eyebrows
and look at Sahir as if to say, 'This father of mine! He can't
be happy till he chases me out of here too.' If he could
bring himself to say it in front of Sahir, he would have
blurted out, 'This blooming father of mine, must he be
everywhere . . . every time? Must he?' But he respected
Sahir, and Akhtar was Sahir's friend.

Jaadu was Jaan Nisar Akhtar's son but his temperament

was like his uncle's. Like Majaz, he was mercurial. Sahir raised him like a son, and indulged him like a friend. On the days Akhtar would be visiting, Sahir would say, 'Jaadu . . . what a wonderful film at Eros yaar . . . whatsitsname . . . not to be missed . . . go watch it.' And in this way Sahir would manage to avoid all possibilities of a face-off between father and son.

Sahir and Jaadu. The bonds that held them together were quite unique.

Once, Jaadu even gave up on Sahir, and walked out of his house.

'You pamper my father too much. Make him feel too important! Unnecessarily!' Jaadu had said. Sahir had laughed at his accusation. And that was it, the final straw. 'You are like him . . . exactly like him . . . he too laughs at me . . . exactly like this.' It was Jaadu's et-tu-Brutus moment. 'I don't need anybody . . . not him, not you!' he said, and walked out on Sahir.

Jaadu stayed unreachable for a few days. He was a man of honour, and since he was young, his sense of self-respect was a little exaggerated. His nose was often in the air, and his attitude turned a notch higher. God alone knows what he ate, where he slept, how he managed to live during the days he was away.

The story goes that he spent much of his time in a studio. Kamaal Amrohi's production manager was a friend of Jaadu's. Jaadu would while away the evenings with him on the studio floors and sleep the nights away in the production store which was filled to the brim with shooting props and paraphernalia. In that cramped storeroom he found the two *Filmfare* statuettes that Meena Kumari—Kamaal Sahib's wife—had won. Every night after this discovery, he would prop himself in front of a life-size mirror and award himself the trophy. He would pretend to be the presenter and announce the award . . . then pretend to receive the award, gracefully bowing before an imagined audience . . . and then become the audience and applaud himself as well. He refused to think of this as make-believe; he preferred to call these performances his rehearsals. And he rehearsed religiously, every night without fail. He told this story to an interviewer after he had received many a *Filmfare* statuette (engraved with his own name) himself, many years later.

When Jaadu was next seen at Sahir's place, he looked careworn, pale and emaciated. Sahir called out to him affectionately but Jaadu's anger had not evaporated yet.

'I am here just for a bath,' he said, 'that is, if you have no objection.'

'Sure,' Sahir granted him the permission, and then said, 'grab a bite as well!'

'I'll eat anywhere but here. I am not breaking bread with you.'

When Jaadu came out from his bath, Sahir kept a hundred-rupee note on the dining table and begun to run the comb through his sparse hair, searching for words. He was wondering how to ask Jaadu to accept the money. He was afraid of bruising Jaadu's pride. Somehow he did muster the courage to say, 'Jaadu, pick up that hundred-rupee note . . . I'll take it from you later.'

In those days, a hundred rupees might not have been a king's ransom, but it was certainly a princely sum. If you had a hundred-rupee note, you either went to a bank or a petrol pump to break it into smaller notes. Jaadu accepted the note as if he was doing Sahir a favour. 'Fine . . . I will take it . . . but I'll return it the day I get my first salary.'

Javed soon found work as an assistant to Shankar Mukherjee. And it was while working with him that he met and teamed up with Salim Khan. He earned himself a fortune as a scriptwriter thereafter. He would drink like his uncle Majaz, and once drunk, would begin to blabber like Sahir. He would vent his anger, his frustrations against his father. But those hundred rupees he did not return to Sahir. He earned in thousands and then in tens of thousands but he would always tell Sahir, 'I have eaten up your money. You'd better forget about it.'

'Don't you worry, son,' Sahir would invariably retort, 'I will find a way to squeeze it out of you!'

It soon turned into playful banter. The two kept ribbing each other over those hundred rupees until the end, but their friendship stayed intact. Sahir did not have many friends, but was fiercely loyal to those who managed to find their way into his heart. But alcohol had a terrible effect on him; a few drinks and the cussing would begin. He would then strip most of the people bare.

During those days Sahir used to live in Krishen Chander's cottage at Juhu. Om Prakash Ashq, an old friend of his, was rooming with him. One day, in front of me, he asked Sahir in Punjabi, 'Sahir, yaar, a few pegs down and you start abusing everybody . . . why, yaar?'

Sahir replied in Punjabi, 'Yaar . . . ab sharaab naal kuch chatpata tou hona chayinda hai, naa! Now one needs something spicy to munch on with alcohol.'

There was one Dr Kapoor amongst Sahir's friends. A heart patient himself, Dr Kapoor nonetheless was the one who monitored Sahir's deteriorating health. Sahir would often quip, 'Doctor, should I come to see you or should I come to show myself to you?'

That fatal last evening too, when Sahir went to Dr Kapoor's, it was both to see him and to show himself to him—as his well-wisher, concerned for his health, and as his patient, anxious about his own. Sahir now no longer lived at Krishen Chander's place. He had finally constructed his own house and had christened it 'Parchaiyaan' (Shadows). Dr Kapoor was now in a bungalow in Versova. And Jaadu had now become a hugely successful and popular writer. Sahir had come to know that Dr Kapoor was not keeping well. A cardiologist, Dr Seth, was coming to check on him. Ramanand Sagar was there too. Sahir was trying to cheer Kapoor up and he called for a deck of playing cards. He shuffled the deck as he propped himself up on Kapoor's bed. As he was dealing out the cards, Kapoor saw Sahir's face stiffening. He was perhaps trying to suppress his pain. Kapoor called out to him, 'Sahir!'

And then and there Sahir collapsed on the bed. Dr Seth arrived at this moment. He tried his best to revive Sahir but there was nothing he could do. Sahir was long gone. Dr Kapoor was scared witless. Finding him a bundle of nerves and worrying for his health, Ramanand Sagar took him away to his own house.

Sahir's driver Anwar came running in. He took charge of the lifeless body of his employer. Anwar first called up Yash Chopra's house; Sahir and Yash Chopra were quite close. But Chopra was in faraway Srinagar. Anwar then called up Jaadu. Jaadu's driver was not on duty so Jaadu hurried over in a taxi. And in that very taxi he brought Sahir's body to his house, to Parchaiyaan. With Anwar and the taxi-wallah's help he managed to haul Sahir's mortal remains to the first floor where Sahir used to live.

Jaadu did not say a word in the taxi, as if he was shocked into silence. But when he reached home, he simply broke down. He hugged Sahir and wept like he had probably not wept in his entire life. It was around one at night now. Where was he to go? Who all should he call up to break the tragic news to? In the end, Jaadu did nothing. He just sat by the lifeless form of his dear friend. By now, the neighbours had heard about Sahir's death and had begun to trickle in. A neighbour said, 'Place both his hands together on his chest, the body will soon start to stiffen, you will have a problem later.' Jaadu kept crying and kept doing everyone's bidding wordlessly.

As the day broke and the news spread, people began to throng in to pay their last respects to the departed soul. Bedspreads had to be taken out for the people to sit on. Chairs had to be rearranged. Doors had to be opened. Jaadu kept sobbing like a child and running all the chores.

When he came downstairs to make the funeral arrangements he found the taxi driver still there. 'Uff! Why didn't you ask me? How much do I owe you, now?' he said petulantly.

The taxi driver must have been a kindred soul. He folded his hands and said, 'Saab . . . I . . . I didn't stay back for the money. After all this, how could I have gone away into the night?'

Jaadu took out his wallet from his pocket.

The taxi driver shook his head, 'Nahi saab . . . let it be!'

Jaadu nearly screamed, 'Take it! Take this hundred-rupee note . . . just keep it! He did find a way to squeeze out his hundred rupees . . . even in his death!'

And Jaadu disintegrated into tears.

All this happened before they hoisted Sahir's mortal remains up on their shoulders and took him out on his last journey.

Bhushan Banmali

When the tea grew cold for the second time, Santoshji asked the khansama, 'What happened? Bhushan hasn't woken up yet?'

'Not yet! I tried to wake him, though. Called out his name.'

'You think calling out his name is enough? Even if you beat a drum next to his ear he is not going to wake up. Anyway, you brew a fresh cup of tea and lay it out on the lawns. I am going to go and wake him up.'

Bhushan loved his wife Usha and his mother-in-law Santosh Bansal in the same fashion, and with equal intensity. If he was miffed with Usha, he would seek solace in Santoshji. And when he fought with Santoshji, he would shuttle back to Usha. But this time Usha was so upset with him that she had gone away to Madras—so he too went away, to his mother-in-law in Punjab.

Bhushan had both a home and a hearth, but he was

a nomad by nature. Neither could the home make him happy, nor could the hearth keep him tied. One day, he had picked up his jhola and left Delhi and come to me in Bombay. A few books, a few journals—that's all he had in that cloth bag of his. Perhaps there were a few letters and a few photographs over which he had fought with Santosh. The two of them used to bring out a reputed Hindi magazine in Delhi that published poetry. It was called *Nai Sadi*, 'the new century'. He wasn't married to Usha then. Back in those days, Usha was still learning how to paint.

Why he came to Bombay he never ever spoke about.

'Where will you stay?' I had asked him.

'Here, with you,' he had said with an impish grin. 'When you throw me out, then I'll think of where to go next.'

I was effectively rendered speechless.

'You will never go back to Delhi, is that it?'

A long pause, and then he had said, 'Did Krishna ever go back to Mathura once he had left it?'

It wasn't an answer I was expecting. How was I to know what or whom he had left behind in Mathura? All I knew was that he, along with Mrs Santosh Bansal, brought out a monthly magazine in which they had published a few of my poems. And when I was in Delhi, I had spent an afternoon in his office, guzzling beer. They had a huge circle of poet friends. That day, one by one they all kept dropping into his office. The bottles of beer too started popping open one by one. Empty beer bottles were soon all over the floor. A waiter kept serving fried fish and kebabs and vegetable fritters late into the afternoon, and we kept listening to each other's poems in rapt attention. Bhushan wrote in Hindi under the pen name Bhushan Banmali but he read Urdu. He kept getting us all drunk, and kept reading out his poems. Santosh was a great fan of his poems—his personal eulogist. But all through the drinking and reading session, I did not see anybody taking out any money to pay for the beer or the snacks. They must be running a tab at the shop, like most poets do, I thought. Getting things on credit was a sacrilegious thing in my household but an honest and established ritual at Bhushan's.

That was my first meeting with Bhushan, the very first time I saw him. The next time was when he came to Bombay. One evening when I returned home, I found him sitting in my room, sipping beer. I walked in and asked my servant, 'Where did the beer come from?'

'Sahib gave me some money and asked me to fetch it.'

I lived in a one-bedroom apartment. It was my home and my office too. I am hostage to a few non-poetic habits—I go to bed early, and am up very early as well. But Bhushan was in the habit of sleeping late into the day. Soon, this began to irk me. To make matters worse, he would often bolt the door from the inside. We would bang on the door, thump on it, do everything short of breaking the door down, but he just wouldn't get up. Frustrated, I finally resorted to unscrewing all the bolts and all the locks from each and every door.

One day, I finally did ask him, 'What's up with *Nai Sadi*?'

'Passed away.' He was as laconic as he could be.

'What do you plan to do now?'

'Whatever you say.'

I was rendered speechless once again.

Bhushan started working with me. Neither as an assistant, nor as an understudy—but as a partner, sort of. There would be debates over J. Krishnamurti. History would be read and then repeated. In one such expansive mood, we even scribbled a letter and mailed it to the Pope: now that science has proved that the earth revolves around the sun, shouldn't he at least extend a papal pardon to Galileo? I don't know whether the letter reached the Pope or whether he ever read it, but when some ten or fifteen years later the papacy issued a formal pardon to Galileo, Bhushan and I rang each other up in congratulatory celebrations.

Then for a long time we ceased to be in touch—Bhushan had started to live on his own, and meanwhile I had got married. One day, Bhushan brought back Usha from Delhi as his lawfully wedded wife. Santosh too would often frequent his place, and it never went down well with Usha. Theirs was a pretty strange relationship— mother and daughter fought with each other over Bhushan. Each claimed him to be hers alone. Each thought the other had encroached upon her relationship with him. And Bhushan—he kept himself engrossed in his reading and writing. Whenever we met we would reminisce about the day we got bitten by wanderlust: 'Bhai, remember that night at Joshimath?'

Wandering through hills and valleys we had finally reached Rudraprayag—Bhushan, Taran Taaran and I. We did not have a driver; I was driving the car myself. We parked and went out for a stroll in the bazaar. When we saw fresh fruits, we bought some; then we saw fresh vegetables and bought some of those too.

That made Taran ask, 'What are we going to do with all this? And so much fruit—who's going to eat all of it?'

'Why don't you just let us buy them first—we don't necessarily have to eat them. Have you ever seen such lush green vegetables and such fresh fruits in Bombay?' Bhushan snapped, biting into a hot jalebi.

'We will give them to the cook at the dak bungalow where we will stay the night.'

In the upper reaches of the Himalayas, the dak bungalows were the only places to stay. Built by the British, you found these dak bungalows everywhere. Pity, nobody builds them any more.

The evening was far away. We had time on our hands. We thought of venturing a little further than what we had planned—to Anandprayag. We knew of a dak bungalow there where we could spend the night. When we returned to our parked car, a Sardarji greeted us, 'Where are you people going?'

The roadworthiness of a travelling car cannot be hidden. And in the hills, it is not difficult to guess your destination—the direction in which the car is parked on the narrow winding roads is a dead giveaway. We told him that we were intending to drive up to Anandprayag.

'If there's space, will you give me a lift?'

'Where do you want to go?'

'Drop me at Anandprayag. My home's there.'

A man is forever in search of a co-traveller. We asked him to join us.

The Sardarji had a very cheerful disposition. His name was Bhola Singh Sandhu, but he called himself B.S. Sandhu. He was from the army and was heading home. The bridge that would take us straight into Anandprayag was under repairs—we had to drive into the city via a drooping, flagging detour. Sandhu saab requested to be dropped there, and like a good Hindustani invited us over to his house. He kept insisting that we come home with him and have dinner: 'You'll not find an eatery here, the further up the road you go, the more difficult it will be to get anything to eat. Please have dinner with me and then go.' But we excused ourselves. The sun had already crept behind the hills.

By the time we reached the dak bungalow it was quite late at night. When we shouted for the caretaker, a chowkidar came out rubbing his eyes. He was in the habit of saying 'no' even before we asked him anything.

'Do you have a vacant room?'

'No.'

'Just for one night?'

'No.'

'How about till five in the morning?'

'No.'

'Has Major Bakshi arrived?' This, in a suddenly authoritative voice.

He just stopped short of saying 'no'. 'Which Major sahib?'

'Major Bakshi had made a booking for today. What about that?'

He turned to look at me but before he could say anything, I issued him an order, 'Go, heat some water. Major sahib is about to arrive. Where's the register, show it to us.'

Rattling under the barrage of our questions, the chowkidar stepped back. Bhushan gave him the bag of fruits and vegetables, 'Here. Keep this. Take it home with you in the morning.'

All the rooms in the bungalow were vacant. We had finally found a place to stay. We were pouring ourselves a drink when Bhushan quipped, 'All we have are these biscuits . . . dunk them in your whiskey—there's nothing else to eat.'

At that very moment a local hill man arrived with a tiffin-carrier: Sandhu saab had sent some piping hot food for us. This kind of hospitality can only be found in this country, in our Hindustan!

Come morning and as always we once again planned to hit the road. And as always, we had to pick up a sleeping Bhushan and dump him in the back seat of the car. We left at four in the morning. Those days it was our mantra to wake up before the sun was up, greet the sun on the road and roost before the sun would. The previous night, we had decided that there was no point turning back from here. Joshimath was only a few kilometres away. We planned to drive up to Joshimath and then onwards to Badrinath, and if possible drive by Govindghat to go to the Valley of Flowers, hitting the road again only after visiting Hemkund. God only knew when we would be able to come to these hills again and whether there would be anything pristine left in these hills to see. Bhushan readily agreed; Taran Taaran was made to.

Our next stop was Joshimath.

Three quarters of the day had passed and I was driving through bursts of sun and patches of clouds. Taran asked, 'Why don't you employ a driver? You keep driving yourself, all the time.'

'Why? Am I such a bad driver?'

'No no. The thing is—you keep looking this side and that instead of keeping your eyes on the road . . . you know how hilly roads are . . .'

Bhushan burst out laughing, 'Till we pull over for the night, the man's going to keep telling you that . . . look . . . look at the colours flying off his face, he's turning pale . . . "even before flying, his complexion was always pale."' Bhushan decided to take the opportunity to quote Ghalib, twisting his words around to accommodate an epithet from the poet.

We were approaching a dangerous bend on the road and I could hear the honking of a bus coming downhill around the bend. The light of the sun filtering through the thick dense overgrowth of the jungle took on a green hue. Our hearts leapt into our mouths as we negotiated the bend and got our first sight of Joshimath. It had snowed there. There was not a single flake of snow on this side of the valley, but everything appeared white on the other side—like icing on cake.

At Joshimath we slid our car into a vacant spot in the bazaar. But no sooner had we opened the door of the car than we pulled it shut—the bitterly cold air had rushed in to rob us of all warmth. We pulled our shawls tightly around us and wrapped our mufflers across every possible inch of our faces. Thus armoured, we stepped out of the car in search of a roof under which we could spend the night. The bazaar was on higher ground than the residential area; so we marched up the steps, and down the slope. More steps, more slopes. A little ascent here, a bit of descent there. In the hills, climbing down a slope is as knee-breaking an activity as climbing up. That is why the Kashmiris say 'Urjo durkat' (may your knees stay intact) every time a friend or a family member steps out of the house. Finally, at the end of an unending flight of steps, we found an ashram—Birla Ashram.

A pundit at the ashram gave us a place to stay— unlocked a room and got three string cots put up. We were the only ones there. We did not see any other traveller, but all the pundit gave us to keep ourselves warm in the freezing cold were thin mattresses, and thinner durrees and blankets. And he looked pretty unapologetic about it: 'No one comes here in this weather . . . they venture here when it is warmer and then these mattresses and blankets are enough. Moreover, those who come also bring a few things with them. What they do not bring and we do not have, they get from the bazaar. You can get everything there on rent.'

We took punditji's hint, took the room key from him and then once again trotted up the hill to the bazaar. When we reached our car, there was a note on the front windshield, under the wipers. The note read:

A little down the road, at the far end of the bazaar you'll find a petrol pump. A road from the pump will lead you straight to our military camp. Please have dinner with us tonight.

—*B.S. Sandhu*

We were a little taken aback by the note. How did this man whom we had dropped outside Anandprayag get here, we wondered.

Bhushan said, 'He got here the way we did—how else? And then he's familiar with our car, isn't he? Why are you all looking so shocked?'

'But he could have told us if he wanted to come to Joshimath?'

'How could he? You told him that we were going only up to Anandprayag. Coming here was an afterthought. We decided to come here only last night, didn't we?'

That was the end of our wonderment.

We ventured into the bazaar, rented a few thick, cozy mattresses, bought an *angeethi*, a small amount of coal and after making all sundry arrangements to beat the cold, we left for the army mess of Bhola Singh Sandhu.

The jawans of Sandhu's unit had already been informed of our arrival. They went all out to make us feel welcome. They had made a huge fire and we sat around it after dinner. They kept pouring us rum—endless Patiala pegs of rum. They belonged to the Punjab Regiment of the Indian Army and they had a reputation to protect, so we drank like fish. They regaled us with Punjabi poetry rendered in an orthodox Punjabi style. Imagine a lot of Punjabi jokes and Punjabi poetry and then imagine your condition when you hear an incomparable blend of the two. Soon we were rolling on the floor, doubling up in laughter. At the end, the jawans served us gulab-jamuns that they had made. They tied a towel like a bib around Bhushan's neck and put a whole tub of gulab-jamuns in front of him. And Bhushan being Bhushan succeeded in squeezing half the sugary syrup of the gulab-jamuns into his mouth and half onto his clothes.

It was quite late when we left the mess. The streets were unlit, and the cold night was so dark that we could not see our own hands. We began to grope for the flight of steps that would take us to the ashram. There wasn't a man in sight whom we could ask for help. The car headlights were hardly of any use. The wind howled. We crawled back into the car, but Taran was unwilling to get in. A few freezing minutes in the howling wind later we saw a man with a torch. We rushed out of the car and grabbed him. He explained that the flight of steps was just a little down the road and even offered to lead the way. But he only walked a few steps with us. Once he had seen the extent of our drunkenness, he simply switched off his torch and slipped away in the darkness.

Finally, we did see a flight of steps. We were sure that these were the ones we wanted and began our climb down. I was leading the way, feeling every step with my foot, speaking aloud, guiding Bhushan and Taran—step, slope . . . step, slope. Suddenly, I realized that there was no one behind me. Somewhere in the distance, drifting through the darkness, was Taran Taaran's faint voice, 'Step, step . . . slope! Step, step . . . slope!'

After every two steps there was a small gap, a gradient. Taran Taaran was being painstakingly careful in guiding Bhushan.

Somehow, we managed to reach the ashram. Only after the key clicked into the lock could we believe that we had arrived at the right place.

Thankfully, we had made the beds before we left. We tucked Bhushan in and threw a quilt on top of him. It was so awfully cold that whatever we touched seemed to have been taken out of the freezer. We tried to start a fire—heaped some coal in the *angeethi* and tried to use some old newspaper to kindle the flames. But try as hard as we could, the coal would just not catch fire—the paper would flare up and then turn into ashes, all we got were short bursts of light. The coal looked like pieces of ice and was damp to the touch—have you ever tried setting cubes of ice on fire? Our stack of old newspapers and magazines was fast getting depleted. I had now begun to despair, 'Taran, if this continues we will soon have to burn our books to warm ourselves.'

The fire didn't light up, but Taran's eyes sure did. They lit up with a spark. There was a lot of brandy left in the bottle. He went and brought the bottle over. He then lit a paper kindle under the bed of coal and began to pour the brandy on top of it.

'All we want is just one piece of coal to ignite—that's all. One piece will be enough to start a decent fire.'

When the thin stream of brandy hit the bed of coal which was being kindled from below, a beautiful blue fire leapt out. For a few moments the coal turned into dazzling sapphires. The whole thing looked so mesmerizing that you wanted to scoop it up into your hands. The brandy was nearly over. But the effort had paid off: a piece of coal had begun to glow red, drunk on nearly half a bottle of brandy. What more could we ask for? We began stoking the fire, blowing at it from below, fanning it from above. And soon we had a steady fire raging. Pockets of smoke had begun to billow and collect in the corners, though. We had nearly spent half the night trying to turn the black coal red.

We dusted our beds and climbed into them. Hardly had I closed my eyes when Taran softly called me. When I said 'Hoon', he whispered, 'There was a lesson I had read in Matric—that one must not sleep with a coal fire raging in a closed room. Burning coal produces a gas that can knock you unconscious. You may even die. Therefore it is a must that we keep a window or a ventilator open, letting in some oxygen.'

I scanned the room. I could see neither a window nor a ventilator in any direction. We were in a soup.

I looked at Taran, 'Taran yaar, did you have to remember what you read in Matric tonight?'

To comfort me, he added, 'But I don't think there's any danger.'

'Who's going to become unconscious with all this shivering in this cold?' I managed to say—but the restlessness remained.

Taran said again, 'Let's keep the door a little ajar, shall we?'

'All right!'

When I opened the door, the cold air rushed in like a rogue. When I kept the door ajar, just a wee bit ajar, the wind began to whistle like hooligans. We were at our wits' end: we just could not think of a way to stave off the cold and silence our fear. A solution did eventually flash through our minds—to prop a suitcase between the door panels and tie them together. But tie them how? We did not have any string. Finally, we pulled the drawstring out from a pair of pajamas. We stuck a suitcase between the two panels of the door and tied them together. Our fear was a little assuaged but the room once again started growing cold. All this had kept us fairly occupied, but time and again, our thoughts would wander to Bhushan—how was he faring in this gnawing cold? Was he warm enough? He was already holed up under a blanket and a quilt. We threw another quilt on top of him—just to make sure that he stayed warm.

Taran turned on his side again and said, 'The cold air is bouncing off the wall and is going straight in search of Bhushan.'

And then a silence. After another quiet interval it was my turn to break the silence, to say something.

'Taran, as the night is deepening, it's growing colder. I think I am going to throw even my mattress on top of him. God forbid if we find him in the morning like the weaver's son-in-law with his body stiff and his smile frozen.'

Taran kept quiet. I got up, pulled out my mattress and threw it atop Bhushan and made do with just a blanket. The fire in the *angeethi* was beginning to die. Taran got up to throw a handful of coal in the dying fire and also picked up his quilt and put it on top of Bhushan. And then he crept under his mattress and lay down. Somewhere along the way, exhausted as we were, we did not even realize when we fell asleep.

It was obvious that we had slept till late. That morning, Bhushan woke up before us. I turned on my side and saw him stretching himself awake.

'How are you?' I ventured. 'Did you sleep well?'

He yawned and said, 'Yes, I did sleep well. But tell me one thing: why did the two of you keep throwing your stuff on top of me all through the night?'

Taran burst out laughing, 'Hear hear! Hear the man! We stay up half the night worrying to death over him and this is what he says. Now, get out of your bed and fetch us some tea.'

The khansama had prepared a fresh pot of tea and was laying it out in the lawns when he saw Santoshji coming out of Bhushan's room and asked, 'What happened, even you failed to wake him up?'

Santoshji had her face hidden in the folds of her shawl. She sank into the chair and with a violent jerk, she shook her head and said, 'No! He's not going to wake up. Never again!'

And then she stifled her sobs in the folds of her shawl.

II

Feet on the ground, water over your head—
This is the megalopolis
Of Mumbai—

The Stench

'What all didn't we do to get you people out of that squalor—out of the indignity of that ghetto! Nine years . . . for a full nine years we kept at it—we fought and bled to get these cement roofs over your heads . . . to get this place recognized as a civic colony . . . and you have the audacity to say that we have squeezed you into boxes . . .?' A belligerent tone had crept into the voice of the man from the party.

My husband would invariably pick an argument with him: 'You call this place a colony? A civic colony? Looks more like a warehouse crammed to the roof with people . . . you have crated us into parcels . . .'

I sat behind the door, curtained from their arguments. What did a woman like me have to do with their politics? But my husband was not one to cow down.

'Arre sala . . . between two buildings shouldn't there at least be enough room for two handcarts to pass? The

41

way these buildings have mushroomed, people going from this end cannot even walk past someone coming from the other.'

'What you talking, my man Methu? Stop exaggerating. Why two men . . . two police jeeps can pass each other . . . you can measure it any time.'

'Cut it out man, just cut it out . . . keep your hand on your heart . . . yes . . . now tell me, can you put two charpoys in here—gather in a few friends for a round of cards? Can you? Tell me!'

'Now, now, come on . . . the alleyways of Bombay are not meant for charpoys, my friend!'

Come to think of it, the contours of the land around me had changed. There was a time when the bay would flush in just a little water and the land would become wet and muddy like a marsh, half the year round. And for the other half, the sun would scorch the mud and the wind would cover everything with flakes of sun-dried mud. The mud and the dust nurtured everything: a multitude of half-naked children and a horde of mangy, scrawny mongrels—and all of Jaani's cockerels and hens. The kids would strap strings around the pups and drag them around all day long in the mud and the dust. When you saw a mutt with a long neck you could be sure where it had grown up.

But now on this stump of land, the government had built three-storeyed buildings, with twenty-four flats on every floor. In every flat there was a single room, a kitchenette around which skeins of fumes wound themselves like balls of yarns, and a lone tap in the

semblance of a bathroom; the toilets were communal—
two on every floor. There was no need to run with the
water spilling out of your tin can into the open any more,
but the queues still formed. The only difference was the
shape of the queues—they used to form in straight lines
earlier, now they snaked along the staircases.

When they began constructing these buildings, they
dragged out all the shanties and dumped them in the
far corner of the ground, just like the way Gaffar piles
his empty wicker baskets in the bazaar. In Gaffar's pile,
a few rotten vegetables would still remain—unwanted,
unsaleable. And in this pile, rotting children and their
unwanted parents howled and yowled their days away,
scavenging a life under a scorching sun, burrowing
through life like bugs, sponging up the sun and the dew
and whatever else the sky would think of hurling at them,
into their bones. These concrete walls gathered no moss.
The shanties used to be quite green, though.

There used to be a little patch of open ground right
in front of our house where Santosh had planted a few
seeds of bitter gourd. When the saplings sprouted leaves
and began to send out rootlets, she propped them up
with a lattice of bamboo splinters and soon the creepers
leapt across the trellis and covered it with vines of tender
green. A beautiful green wall now separated Santosh's
hut from the next. But a wall of vines was only a wall
of vines. It failed to stave off a neighbour's envy or her
greed—miserably so when temptation sprouted in the
form of pods of bitter gourd that sat enticingly just an
arm's reach away. The moment the pods bloomed, out

would come the neighbour swinging her bucket to wash
clothes by the green trellis. And when eyes wouldn't be
watching, her hand would shoot out and pluck the pods
and conceal them under the mound of washed clothes in
the bucket. She would fry the bitter gourds with some
potatoes and a toss of red chillies. With the chillies you
couldn't even smell the bitter gourd cooking. How would
Santosh ever find out?

But all the same, she had become suspicious. That's
why when Rajjab Ali's garage was pulled down by the
municipality, Santosh's husband got hold of a thin sheet
of aluminium and put it behind the bamboo laths in such
a way that it totally hid the bitter gourd vines. That's how
occasionally the smell of bitter gourds cooking would
drift out from Santosh's house. There was no need for the
aroma to be stifled with red chillies any more. Oh yes, if
you asked her for some bitter gourds she would give you
a few sometimes. Even she took unripe tomatoes from
my flower pots. Everyone had grown something or the
other in front of their shanties. Tulsi plants were there,
of course—watered every morning and evening. No one
knew why the tulsi was planted, why an earthen lamp
was lit under it. Everyone—Amina, Karima, Shanti and
Puro—would say, 'Whenever the old man coughs I give
him tulsi extract.' Some people's vines had crept up the
huts and spread over the roofs.

But Aunty, being Aunty, had constructed a still—right
behind her shack, not like Bakshi who had his distilling
apparatus in the corner of the maidan. Bakshi would
brew liquor only once in ten–fifteen days and distil just

enough to fill his drums. The days Bakshi would fire his still you could see the havildar making rounds of his hut right from the morning. Bakshi owned another two huts—the men of honour would sit inside one of these and drink. And the men of normal stature, whose honour would neither increase nor decrease if they were seen drinking, would squat outside the huts and drink the country liquor. For snacks they would lick the salt kept on the plate in front of them. But Aunty was Aunty—she would distil her alcohol with great love and tenderness. She would put some rotting fruits in her brew and very little sal ammoniac. Her alcohol was the colour of gold. And if you brought in your own empty bottle she would give a discount of one rupee on the price. Her customers were mostly regulars. They were the only ones who came to her and never after 10 p.m. After that it was her time to drink. She would drink herself senseless, feast on beef and then go off to sleep. If somebody were to wake her up, she would hurl such choice abuses at them that the entire basti would become redolent with the language.

But now even Aunty was imprisoned behind walls. You no longer got to hear her—as if her voice has been choked. She did not seem this lonely earlier.

And Jaani . . . these days he says that the money from his hotel job is not enough, not any more. He sold off some of his chickens, ate some and some died. What could he do? You couldn't raise chickens on the second or third floor!

This year, Gaffar did not buy a billy goat either. On Bakr-i-Id, he sacrificed his own she-goat. What else could he do? Earlier he would let his goat loose and the goat would look after herself—she would graze for food somewhere in the rubbish heaps of the basti. Now she was eating away the clothes in the house—the cost of two lungis had got added to Gaffar's monthly budget. Poor Gaffar. When he did not have his pukka house, he was so much better off.

My husband too used to often bring his friends home. He would set the charpoy outside our shack and drink and argue most of the night away; and then they would roll over there itself and sleep through the rest of the night. In the morning they would all get up and go about their duties. Now my husband had stopped bringing his friends over. In these one-room homes, what would all the men and women do now? Earlier the children would lie on the floor inside and the men would sleep outside. The women, after filling their buckets with water from the tap, would come and pick up their bleating kids and wrap them around their bosoms and go off to sleep. What were they to do now? The grown-up kids . . . they all kept staring wide-eyed.

I have told my husband a number of times, 'Damn it, is this any life? The government had locked us up in boxes and you know why . . . so that the stench of poverty stays contained, stays inside. Come, let's sell this pukka house and go somewhere else . . . to some other slum. Surely we can find some place that we like.'

The Rain

The rain was unrelenting. It had poured night and day, continuously, for five days in a row. And Damoo had been drinking relentlessly, day and night, all through those five days, competing with the downpour. Neither would the rain let up nor would Damoo let go. The steadfast rain and stubborn Damoo. Drunk, both.

Damoo had always been like this. When he picked up the bottle he had to completely take to it. His drinking bouts stretched into days, going on for twenty days, sometimes thirty. He would drink all through the day and right through the night. When his wife stopped Laksha from supplying him more, Damoo would conjure up a bottle from anywhere—from under the mattress, from inside the containers in the kitchen, even from the rafters on the roof. He had an insatiable capacity to drink. And he was happy when he was drinking. He was never the man you would find in a drunken brawl;

47

in this Damoo was quite unlike others. And when he gave up the hooch, he really gave it up—he wouldn't touch the devil for three or four months at a stretch, sometimes even for a full six months. When he was on the wagon, there wasn't another man like him in the basti—there was no better father than him, no better husband, no better worker.

But all that was in another season. Seasons change. This monsoon he had started drinking with the very first showers. And this year it wasn't raining, it was pouring. Such a downpour had not been seen in the last hundred years.

The city braved the first day of the onslaught. Local train services were suspended, then resumed, and then suspended again. The second day took its toll—trucks were unable to enter the city. They started grinding to a halt on the highways. The city was flooding. The supply of fresh vegetables dried up. Prices shot up like the ears of a rabbit. The rain kept falling—in sheets. Steadily, unfalteringly. And Damoo kept drinking, matching the intensity of the rain.

By the third day the signs of danger were loud and clear. Rain and more rain accompanied by strong winds. The wind drove the sheets of rain into the lane, and it quickly started filling up. Half the household lay strewn outside Damoo's house in the lane—his wife started dragging it all into the kholi, their one-room tenement. The kholi had the wingspan of a sparrow. It could hardly accommodate Damoo, his wife Shobha, and their daughter Kishni who was to be married off the next month. When the wife pulled in the family goat as well, Damoo lost it: 'Abey, what's the need to get this behen inside?'

'What am I to do—let it soak in the rain? Till when?'

'Look at the bloody thick coat she has! She's not going to wilt in two hours.'

'You say two hours, but it's been two days. Today the lane's flooded. Even the drain's spilling over. I think this accursed rain is going to sweep Punya's shanty away.'

Damoo fell silent. He smacked a little salt off his right hand, picked up the glass and guzzled half a glass of hooch. The booze scorched his innards and he belched out a thick, filthy curse—directed this time at the maker of the hooch.

'The bastard. Saala has poured so much naushader* into the booze it tastes more like battery acid.'

Shobha did not respond. She tied the goat in the corner and spoke to Kishni instead. 'Get up beti. Pick up all the things from the floor and put them on the shelf. I'm afraid some water will seep in. This rain is not going to let up. It has started raining harder instead . . .'

She hadn't even finished speaking when a clamour rose in the streets, 'Look at that, that's Punya's shanty— it . . . it's gone.'

Shobha looked out of her door: Muqadam's roof had collapsed and slid onto the lane. People ran across to hoist it up again, but there was no point. Instead of flowing in from the lane, the water was now filling in from the top. The sky was stubborn in its intent.

---

*Ammonium chloride

Kishni wanted to run out, to help, but Shobha stopped her: 'You stay put. You're going to get married next month. I don't want you to break a limb.' She muttered something more under her breath and hurried out of the house.

Damoo looked at his daughter. There were now only the three of them—Damoo, Kishni and the goat. Love for his daughter was spilling out of his bosom. He wanted to reach out to her, to strike up a conversation.

'Are there any onions in the house, beti? Will you give me one—sliced? Sprinkle some salt on it.'

Kishni began to slice an onion without a word. And Damoo scooped up the bottle of booze from the window and filled his glass all over again.

'Pour me a glass of water too, from the *matki*.'

Without saying anything, Kishni filled a mug with water and gave it to her father. Damoo now had half a glass of booze topped to the brim with water. Kishni had walked back to her corner of the room before Damoo could extend his quivering hand over her head in blessing. The hand kept flapping in the air for a few orphan moments, quite like a bird in mid-flight, and then came down to roost.

'You no worry, beti. I'll arrange your marriage with style. Will give you twenty-five thousand rupees kholi, another twenty–five thousand for clothes and jewellery. And also give your man twenty-five thousand cash. Full one lakh I'll bring. Will spend all on your marriage. One lakh, too much, no? All right, fifty thousand then. I'll get fifty thousand for your marriage.'

He must have said this at least twenty-five thousand times, this talk of fifty thousand rupees. Every time Shobha would snub him, 'Where from? Where will you bring the money from—bet on a race or do a dacoity or what?'

This was what Shobha told him every time. And he too, in every drunken stupor of his, would put his hand in blessing over his daughter's head in his own inimitable style and repeat the exact same words, 'You no worry, beti . . .'

Kishni put down the plate of sliced onions and salt and moved out of Damoo's sight. The floodwater had by now started seeping into the house. The bucket in the kitchen was still ringing with raindrops trickling in from the leaking roof. The goat had been squatting on the floor. It now stood up on all fours.

Shobha was not yet back. It had been quite some time. Kishni had braved the rain and ventured out to find her mother. She too had now been gone for over half an hour. Damoo began to worry about their possessions.

The first thing he secured was his litre of booze: he put it on a higher shelf. The other bottle was still safe, hidden inside a canister of daal in the kitchen. Then he filled a jug with water and kept it safely aside. After that he hauled the two tin trunks up on the wooden plank that also doubled up as their bed. The third trunk proved too heavy for him. He hurt his feet trying to drag it up—so he let that be.

The goat stood crouched in a corner in silent prayer. Damoo found some puffed rice in a jar, filled some into

his pockets, scooped some in his hands and returned
to where he had been sitting—and continued drinking
and munching. The kholi was now fast filling up with
floodwater.

Now, Shobha returned, but not Kishni. She had hitched
her sari over her knees. She yelled, 'Listen, today no
cooking possible at home. Maliya's hotel is flooded, half-
filled with water. People are running for shelter to the
garages on the upper side.'

He was drunk but he remembered, 'What about
Muqadam—his house, flooded or no?'

'Poor man! He's still at it, hauling his stuff upstairs
to safety. Everybody's at it—Heera, Gopal, Sulaiman,
everybody. But what to do—look after the young and
the old or save the belongings?'

Shobha was picking up the foodstuff and keeping
them aside safely, one by one. She had brought some
vada-pav for Damoo. As she was giving it to him, she
kept on the prattle, 'How many kids these people in our
mohalla produce? At least ten kids you'll find in every
size. Thank God, we only have one.'

Damoo was relieved to see his wife back. He shook
the droplets of rain from his hair and said, 'If you could
have held on to your pregnancies, here also would be a
long line of kids.'

Shobha glared at him, 'There is a God above, no, to
save me. Here . . . eat it.'

Damoo grabbed her wrist, 'Why, God's your relative
or what?'

'Let go of me!' Shobha said in mock irritation. 'Be ready

to leave . . . just look how fast the water's filling up.'

Shobha had propped a chair on top of the two trunks. Damoo quietly stood up and climbed atop the chair, 'This high your relative cannot come also. Forget the water.'

'Be careful! Don't fall down. There won't be anybody here to pick you up.'

'Why? Where are you going?'

'To the roof on the garage. They need help. Even Kishni's there.'

'When is she coming back?'

'As soon as the rain lets up we will all return.'

But this time round nobody let up—neither the rain nor Damoo. The floodwater in the lane kept surging. The drain metamorphosed into a river. Muqadam's youngest son fell into the water and was swept away. A few people ran to pull him out but the current dragged the boy further away. A few people got wounded in the effort. Some people thought that the boy had got sucked into an open manhole above which the floodwaters had created a whirlpool.

And then the electricity went. Or perhaps the government had shut off the power to stave off electrocutions from short circuits. As the day began to wear off the city begun to drown in darkness as well. The three garages on the upper side of the lane got filled with six feet of water. The cars, stripped of their engines for repair, were floating in the water like graves. There were a number of huge floor-to-ceiling cabinets in the garage. People threw out the stuff from the shelves closest to the ceiling and crawled into them. No one had any intention of stepping down till the rain abated.

Those who could escape sought shelter on the roofs of sturdier buildings, in hospital verandas, in school classrooms. Kishni was sitting lifelessly in a hospital veranda. Somebody had broken the news to her—they said Shobha was seen drowning in the floodwater; a few others said that she had been bitten by a snake. A number of serpents had been seen swimming in the deluge.

While there still was some daylight left, a couple of young men did venture to enter Damoo's kholi. But they could not break in. The water now reached up to their necks. The goat hung in the water, legs up, in the doorway. It was long dead. The undercurrent near the wall was strong, and the window at the back was totally under water. Damoo had somehow managed to pull the other table—on which Shobha kept their utensils—up on their bed. A few pots and pans were still floating in the water. Most had been swept away. The roar of the rain and the gurgle of the surging water threatened to split their eardrums. The young men called out for Damoo, yelled his name till they were hoarse, but Damoo—a bottle in one hand and a long wooden stick in the other—was busy trying to fish out a few floating tomatoes and cucumbers from the water. He was actually fishing—hooking them and then reeling them in. And he was laughing. He neither heard them call out to him nor did he call out for help. Perhaps he had not even thought of seeking help—he was still above the water, he was still in the race, the bet was still in play: who would let up first—the rain or Damoo.

The Charioteer

The first steamboat to Elephanta Caves left the piers of Gateway of India at seven-thirty in the morning. That was why Maruti had to be there by six-thirty. His chores were well-defined: sweep the boat, pick up the litter of last night's passengers and finally wash and mop it clean; then move on to the next boat. That was what his mornings were all about, that was his routine.

Narasingha Rao, his employer, was happy with his work but he had the foulest mouth one could possess—he had no control over his tongue, swearing out a litany of profanities. Agreed, he did not mean a single one of the foul words he spat out, but each of his foul utterances did rankle in Maruti's ears and singe his heart nonetheless. Narasingha Rao's lungi was hitched high up on his thighs and there was a six-finger-wide tilak on his forehead, freshly anointed. He must be waking up his god pretty early in the morning.

By the time the boat was all washed up and clean, a motley crowd of passengers would have queued up for the ride. Tourists from abroad, mostly American and Japanese, herded in groups by their travel agents. Quite often the passengers for the first boat ride strolled out of the Taj Hotel right in the front of the pier, clutching onto their small little bags, an assortment of hats on their heads, cameras and binoculars slung across their shoulders. But the peace with which Maruti cleaned the first boat would go missing when he started work on the second one. No sooner would the first boat leave than the passengers left behind would jump into the second one, even before he could finish his mopping. And to add to his woes, the passengers for the second boat would be of a different kind—less classy, more demanding. Gone would be the meaningless swearing of the morning, the gentle cursing. The cussing now developed a sting— Maruti could feel it whiplash against his skin—worsening as the sun became stronger.

Narasingha Rao owned three ferries. They trawled the waters between Gateway and Elephanta—filled their bellies with passengers on one shore and emptied them at the other, leaving in their wake crumpled, empty packets of spicy savouries, shells of peanuts, peels of oranges, wrappers of chocolates and candies, vomit, angrily tossed packets of contraceptives, beads from a broken necklace, somebody's cap and another's handkerchief. Maruti's arms would tire picking up the trash.

The passengers were not allowed to throw anything overboard into the sea, but Maruti never ever stopped anyone from doing so. If they insisted in their own ways to lessen his burden, lighten his load, who was he to stop them? Scraping the dried vomit from the floor of the boat was the hardest thing to do. And it was very common for those travelling in a boat in the sea for the first time to puke; it was the common curse—the shared disease. Most people leant against the railings and puked over them, and in their effort to do so, puked mostly on their own shirts and onto the benches. It was worse during high tide. All that they had eaten would come out. Narsingha Rao had issued a standing order to scoop water up from the tank and clean the vomit immediately. It was back-breaking work and Maruti would double up in pain. At times he would even be kicked by the superior. On these ferries he was the lowliest of the low—he was the *mehtar*, a mere sweeper. So they would ask him to do whatever they liked. The captain of the boat brought his lunch in a box but ate with proper plates and cutlery. And Maruti had to clean both his tiffin box and his plates and then arrange his basket before he left in the evening.

For ten, continuous hours he maintained his balance on a boat rolling on the waves of the sea; by the time the boat anchored at the harbour, every single bone in his body would be aching. He would be left with hardly any energy to clean the boat.

Narasingha Rao cussed at Maruti's mother lewdly and swore at him: 'Why don't you clean the boat now itself . . . otherwise in the morning you will have to slog your own sorry ass!'

Maruti did not even have the energy to answer him. He gestured to say, 'In the morning . . . no breath left right now.' His limbs felt lifeless.

Pushed, shoved through the multitudes of crowds, scraping through somehow, he reached Churchgate Station and managed to board the local; his shoulders drooped, his eyes begun to close. At Jogeshwari, the crowds spat him out of the train. It was a daily ritual.

Somehow, gathering every little bit of energy, he staggered on to the hillock near the highway into kholi number 109 of shanty-town Sawant Nagar. Tulsibai, like every other day, filled the shining bowl with water from the kalsi and thrust it into his hands, saying, 'Tired? Here, have this.'

He propped himself up on his elbows and drank the water in one swoop, washing it down his throat.

Tulsi came and sat by him on the bed and, pressing his aching feet, narrated the happenings of the day.

Laxmi had come from her sasural . . . her in-laws had gone to Nasik.

Maruti closed his eyes. A moment passed. Tulsi said once again, 'Chotti has become wicked . . . imagine, she called me Nani! And she was calling you by your name, asking you when you are going to come . . . lisping, stuttering and all, "When will Maluti come? When?"'

A smile broke across Maruti's careworn face, the tiredness on his features rearranged itself into a smile.

'She speaks in Hindi!'

'Oh yes!'

'Hasn't learnt Marathi!'

'She will! There's still time.'

The tiredness of the day began to creep away. He rested his head on his folded arms.

'How did she go back?'

'She didn't . . . they have gone to see a film.'

'Chotti also?'

'The little devil does not let go of her mother for even a moment. What was she to do? So they took her along.'

Maruti grunted and took a deep breath.

'And Karthik? Where's he?'

'Today he again fought with someone at school!'

'Mother of . . .!'

Maruti turned on his side and abruptly got up.

'Bloody idiot, every day he gets beaten up at school and comes . . . bloody coward. Ghati. He is a disgrace to the Marathas!'

Tulsi also got up.

'Go . . . freshen up . . . I've made some poha . . . have a little.'

Maruti pulled down a towel and lowered himself into a corner to have a bath. 'Take out my dhoti–kurta,' he said.

The stove was lit. The lamp too was switched on. Maruti folded his hands in front of the idols kept there, murmured some words of prayer and put on his fresh dhoti–kurta.

Karthik walked in. Maruti jumped on Karthik, put a hand between his legs and threw him against the bed and pressed him under himself.

'Come, you idiot. Come wrestle with me!'

It tickled Karthik.

Maruti said, 'From tomorrow get yourself massaged with mustard oil, go to the *akhara* and train yourself to wrestle. You will achieve nothing by reading books and being a Gyandev!'

Karthik kept laughing. Despite the gushing noise of the kerosene stove, Tulsi could hear everything and said, 'Why are you teaching him stupid stuff . . .?'

'I'm teaching him the right stuff. A Maratha's son has to be a brilliant Maratha!'

Babu arrived now outside the door and called for him to come outside the kholi.

'What say, Maruti? Want to come along for Patkar's meeting?'

Maruti said from inside the kholi, 'Holy shit, do you have any idea why people go for that meeting? My wife says that all you do there is scratch your balls.'

From inside the kitchen Tulsi cussed at the two. 'Woe be upon you, bastards!'

Maruti moved out.

'You heard what my bai said?'

After the meeting at the local brewery, they argued. From Baba Ambedkar to Medha Patkar, from Chavan to Pawar, they discussed everyone and analysed everything threadbare.

In the middle of the night when a couple of drunks shattered the silence of the alley, Tulsi got up from the cot. She lit the stove and began to warm the food again. Her son-in-law was sleeping on a cot in the alley. Maruti's cot too was laid next to him. Maruti stepped inside laughing. Karthik was sleeping on the wooden bed. Laxmi too was asleep, the little one cradled next to her. Maruti put his hand over the child's head and pinched her cheeks and tried to mimic her lisp: 'Maluti's come.'

Tulsi scolded him, 'Let her be. Don't you wake her up now.'

Laxmi woke up. She hugged the father. Chotti also woke up. Karthik turned on his side and muttered: 'Bapu!' The son-in-law bent down to touch his feet.

Now, Maruti wasn't the lowliest of the low ... not a mere *mehtar*; he was the captain of his family: the charioteer steering a seven-horse chariot!

From the Footpath

The same dog bit Dagroo once again—for the third time. He could not fathom what kind of scent his body gave off that made Shendy so mad. Shendy was the name of the dog.

Behram said, 'It's a stench bey, not a scent that comes out of your body. The poor dog just can't bear it.'

'Why the hell does he sleep next to me every night then?' Dagroo protested. 'I keep chasing him away but sometime during the night the bastard comes and buries his head into me and goes off to sleep.'

Something in the way he said it tickled Hira and she began to laugh. Uninhibitedly. She said, 'Three times. That's once too many. Next time, *you* bite him.'

In this part of the neighborhood, on this footpath of Bandra, Hira was one of a kind. She would be up before the sun and within a couple of hours she would scavenge more than half the garbage cans in Khar and

was not the same man—Sita's death had taken its toll on him, something inside him had broken. Earlier he would hover around her, snuggle against her all night long, whereas now he disappeared for nights on end without a trace. He had begun to chase the occult, seek refuge in the mystic and the magical. She had heard that he had found a group of tantric men— practitioners of black magic. She had no idea what he was looking for, all she knew was that he had started to remember Sita often.

Twelve months later, Hira returned to her life on the footpath in Bandra. She did not say why. The wound on Dagroo's leg had festered. His entire leg was one huge putrid infection.

Behram said, 'Abey go . . . get yourself treated at the municipal hospital. Get yourself pricked with some injection or whatever or else one day you will end up barking.'

But Dagroo did not go.

Hira too said, 'Go man, go to the hospital or else one day you will have to get your leg sawed off.'

And that's what happened.

Hira was with him the day they sawed his leg off. They sedated him first and then it took him an entire day to come back to consciousness. When he came to his senses he cried a lot. They kept him in the hospital for twenty-five full days. Hira told him, 'Believe it or not, but Shendy sat outside the hospital the entire length of those twenty-five days.'

When Dagroo came back from the hospital, Hira settled down with him and Shendy. Once again, Hira had

got a few blackened and dented aluminum pots and pans and had put together a few bricks to fire up a kitchen in a corner. And she had begun to cook for Dagroo. She had once again begun to get up before the sun. And once again she had begun to scavenge more than half the garbage cans in Khar and Bandra.

And then, one day, Shendy somehow managed to get run over by a speeding car. It pained them both. Hira cried her heart out. Then she said, 'Bheeku too . . . he too died the same way.'

Dagroo asked, 'What happened?'

'He had got up to pee in the middle of the night. He was crossing the road, towards the railway lines. And then suddenly from the other side a car came. Very fast . . . it knocked him down . . . and ran over him as he fell . . . the bastard did not even stop . . . just sped away . . . the municipality van came in the morning . . . inquired around . . . but I did not say anything . . . what was I to do . . . who would want to get involved with the police . . . and then who would go and cremate his body . . . the municipality van dragged him away . . . the same way they dragged Shendy away . . . this is how damned life is on the footpath!'

III

Dreams heed no borders, the eyes need no visas
With eyes shut I walk across the line in time
All the time—

III

LoC

The army had more or less encamped permanently at the border in the wake of the 1948 skirmish. Camps gave way to barracks and even the floors of the bunkers got cemented. In less than fifteen years it had become a ritual—the arrivals, settling-downs and departures of army troops. By 1965, life at the border had its own regime, developed its own rhythm. Political harangues, caustic diatribes and cross-border firing had become routine. It was normal for soldiers to open fire across the Line of Control whenever a minister was visiting a border outpost. At times they would sally into the villages across the border and grab a few lambs or goats. Those nights they would feast their guest on purloined loins. Nobody would be censured. None of it would raise any eyebrows.

But God forbid if civilians got caught in their crossfire—now that would certainly make news. The newspapers would scream out in provocative headlines, and politicians would find fodder for their inflammatory speeches. The LoC would smoulder like a live wire.

But there would be times when all would be quiet on all fronts—a long interval when the guns would fall silent. An eerie silence would fall on the border and it would seem as if all ties between the two countries had been snapped, as if all relationships had gone cold. And then to resume their old ties, there would be an incendiary display of fireworks over a few days. Warmth would return to their veins all over again. A count of fatalities would creep into the headlines: five dead on this side and seven killed on the other. Just a statistical log of debit and credit across the LoC in a ledger.

The distance between the bunkers on either side was not much. Sometimes even this distance would disappear: some lissom, lovelorn soldier tucked in a hillock on the other side would belt out a *mahiya* in a plaintive note—

Do pattar anara de
O my beloved
For once come into my lane
For once inquire
How this sick man is faring . . .

And the soldiers on this side would sing a retort—

Do pattar anara de
How to reach you
O my beloved,

There are guards all around you
Of your wicked suitors.

The hillocks that faced each other across the border were just a shoulder apart, so close together that if they stooped they would be hugging each other. The *azan* from that side could be heard on this side, and from this side on the other. Once Major Kulwant Singh had even asked his junior captain, 'Oye, the *azan* was heard just a little while ago, wasn't it? Why is there an *azan* again after half an hour?'

Majeed had begun to laugh, 'This time it is from the other side, sir. The Pakistani time is thirty minutes behind us, you see.'

'So, whose *azan* do you follow to the prayers?'

'Whichever one suits me on that particular day, sir.' Captain Majeed had clicked his heels together, saluted the major and walked off.

Kulwant thought that there must be something about young Majeed that he had become so pally with him so soon. His smile seemed to suggest he had grown up holding his hand.

One night, Majeed sought his permission to enter his tent and placed a tiffin carrier on the teapoy.

'What is it?'

'Mutton, sir. Homemade.'

Kulwant kept the glass on the table and stood up.

'Great! How come? What's the occasion?'

'Bakr-i-Id, sir! This is the sacrificial lamb. You will have it, sir?'

'Yes, yes . . . why not?' Kulwant opened the tiffin carrier himself and picking up a piece of the roasted mutton, said, 'Make yourself a drink.'

'No sir, thank you!'

'Come on. Make a drink. Id mubarak!'

With the mutton chop dangling from his fingers, he embraced Majeed thrice.

'Once upon a time, Fattu Masi would roast these delicately for us. Mushtaq's ammi. Long ago in Saharanpur.' He looked at Majeed, 'Have you ever savoured *ghuggni* made of black chickpeas along with mutton roast? It is simply to die for.'

Majeed wanted to say something but checked himself. Then with some deliberation he said, 'This roast has been sent over by my sister.'

'She lives here? In Kashmir?'

'Yes sir. In Kashmir, but . . .' His voice trailed off.

'But what?'

'She lives in Zargul . . . on the other side.'

'Arre!' Kulwant was sucking the marrow from a succulent bone which he held in his right hand as he poured a drink for Majeed from his left, 'Cheers! Once again, Id mubarak!'

After he clinked his glass with Majeed's, he asked him, 'So, how did your sister send this across?'

Majeed could feel the air stiffen a bit. He began to feel a little uncomfortable. Kulwant asked him with stringent military precision, 'Did you go over to the other side?'

'No, sir! I've never been. Not even once.'

'Then?' The word hung in the air.

'My brother-in-law's the lieutenant commander on the other side. My sister came over to meet him.'

Kulwant picked up his glass and sipped his whiskey. It had grown warm now. He slapped the tiffin carrier shut and stood authoritatively in front of Majeed. 'How did you manage to bring this across? What's the bundobast between the two of you?'

Majeed kept quiet.

'What was the bundobust?' Kulwant thundered.

'In the village below, there are a lot of men whose houses are on this side but their farms on the other,' Majeed began to stutter in answer. 'There are men in a similar situation in villages on the other side too whose houses and farms are thus divided. Families and relations too. So . . .'

Kulwant Singh had more faith in Majeed's voice than the words he had cobbled together. A pregnant pause—and then when Kulwant put some more roast on his plate, Majeed said, 'The commander on the other side is a friend of yours, isn't he, sir? I know because I have read an article that you had written.'

Kulwant Singh froze. There was only one name that cropped up in his mind. And when Majeed spoke the name, tears welled up in his eyes.

'Mushtaq Ahmad Khokar . . . from Saharanpur.'

Kulwant's hands began to shake. He walked up to the window in his tent and looked outside. A few soldiers were crossing the camp in step with each other.

Majeed spoke softly, 'Commander Mushtaq Ahmad is my sister's father-in-law.'

Kulwant turned sharply, 'Father-in-law? Oye, your sister's married to Naseema's son?'

'Ji.'

Kulwant blurted out, 'Oye you . . .'

Major Kulwant Singh began to choke on his own words. He picked up his glass and scoffed the whiskey down his throat as if he was trying to swallow the lump that was there.

Mushtaq and Kulwant both belonged to Saharanpur. Once upon a time they had both studied together at the Doon College. And they had both trained together at the Doon Military Academy. Their mothers—Mushtaq's ammi and Kulwant's beji—were fast friends. And then the country was partitioned—and along with the country the army was divided too. Mushtaq went over to the other side with his entire family, and Kulwant stayed behind. Thereafter the two families had had no contact with each other.

A few days later, Kulwant walked a few miles from the camp along with a junior officer named Vishwa and made him establish radio contact with the commander on the other side. Mushtaq was a little taken aback. But once he got over his surprise, the two friends began to sling such choice profanities and obscenities at each other in their native Punjabi that their hearts opened up and their eyes began to water. When Kulwant finally found his breath, he asked, 'How's Fattu Masi?'

Mushtaq said, 'Ammi has grown very old now. She had invoked Khwaja Moinuddin Chishti for a *mannat* and all she wants now is to go to Ajmer Sharif and offer a chador on his shrine with her own hands. But Rabiya cannot leave the children alone to go with her . . . I just keep blabbering, you probably don't have the foggiest idea who Rabiya is.'

'Of course I do. Majeed's sister . . . that's Rabiya, right?'

'How do you know that?'

'Majeed's my junior, bhai.'

'Oye . . . oye . . .' and another torrent of obscenities ensued.

'Take good care of him,' Mushtaq said in an emotionally charged voice.

Then the two of them decided that Mushtaq would bring his mother to the Wagah border where Kulwant's wife Santosh would meet up with her. Santosh would then bring her over to their house in Delhi. She would take her on a pilgrimage to Ajmer Sharif, and then to meet Beji in Saharanpur. Wouldn't the two old women just love to spend a few days together? To Mushtaq it seemed that a huge load had been heaved off his chest.

Then one day, a message arrived from Mushtaq: ammi's visa has come through. Kulwant called up his wife to fix the date for her to come to the Wagah border. All arrangements were made. All that was left was to inform Mushtaq.

And that was the day that the defence minister landed up at the outpost and guns began to sound on both sides of the border. Kulwant knew that this was only a matter of a few days—this too would pass. He may not be able to contact Mushtaq over the wireless in this situation but he could always send across a villager from below with the message; Majeed had the resources. But yet, Kulwant could not stop himself from worrying. Santosh would say that now even Beji had started calling from the local post office and had started shooting questions. 'Ni . . . Fattu's coming, right? Will you be able to reach Wagah on your own? Will you be able to recognize her or do you want me to come along?'

Majeed reported, 'Sir, the Pakistanis have started heavy shelling.'

Kulwant was already irritated, '*Khasma nu khaaye Pakistan* . . . to hell with Pakistan, what about Fattu Masi?'

On the fifth day of August, Pakistani forces attacked Chambh and crossed the Line of Control. On the twenty-eight day of August, Indian troops captured the Haji Pir Pass, eight kilometres into Pakistan-occupied Kashmir.

On that very day, on 28 August 1965, Fattu Masi was making mutton roast and Beji was boiling black chickpeas for *ghuggni* when the news arrived—eleven Indian soldiers had attained martyrdom at the LoC. Amongst them was one Major Kulwant Singh.

Over

Bujharat Singh had got so used to talking over the wireless radio that he would suffix all his conversations with 'Over'. We were standing just next to him and he said, 'Why don't you pull that charpoy and sit? Over!'

We pulled up the charpoy and sat. Gopi whispered into my ears, 'Bujharat Singh! Now, what kind of a name is that?'

I shrugged my shoulders, 'It is, so it is. So leave it be.'

Bujharat Singh had been speaking for quite some time now over a wireless radio, 'Put four–five beefy burly men on his back and make the bugger run . . . he will automatically fall in line. Over!'

The wireless set cackled. Bujharat Singh lit up his beedi and puffed in the smoke. The party on the other side said something and Bujharat Singh snapped, 'Rope his legs together . . . then chase him with a stick . . . make him run . . . a kos at least. Over!'

He breached his talk to listen and then picked up the wireless radio and barked into it, 'Arre, you will get nothing by starving him. He will die, uselessly. You also, no, talk like a stupid man sometimes. Over!'

He was doling out advice to somebody in another camp on how to rein in a crazed camel. A lantern lit his face amidst the darkness gathering in the sand dunes. Gopi and I sat patiently on the other side of the lantern. We were at a desert outpost, about forty kilometres from Pochina.

Pochina is situated at the India–Pakistan border. We were here on a film shoot. You could not really call Pochina a village. It was more like a outpost flung out in the desert, a pastiche of houses huddled together—but quite picturesque, like houses drawn in crayon in a children's drawing book. The garrison quarters too was not a pukka building, but a framework of bricks plastered with mud. There were two rooms—barrack-like—and a square alcove cut into one wall. A soldier in full military regalia stood in the alcove leaning on his gun—quite pointlessly—while the rest of his garrison romped about in their undershirts and *gamchas* doing squats or massaging each other bare-bodied, slathering mustard oil onto their rippling muscles. Poor men! With the arrival of our heroine, they had to comb their hair and strain themselves into proper clothes.

And what a location our director had dug up! Scenic! There were ridges upon ridges of desert sand wherever you looked, as far as the eye could see. Undulating in the wind—now a crease here, now a crescent there.

About two furlongs from this outpost was a cement milestone. 'Bharat' was written on one side of the stone and 'Pakistan' on the other. Such milestones are hammered into the sandy earth along the border at an interval of two furlongs. Between the two milestones the land lies barren—just a patchy growth of puny scrub which sheep and camels keep scratching at. These animals roam about with full freedom on either side of the border, unburdened by religion, unfettered by boundaries of nation-states. You cannot make out the religion or the nationality of their owners either.

We had a permit to be there for three days. And we also had the permission to pitch our own tents. But we had a small problem on our hands. The men would crouch behind the dunes for their morning ablutions. But what would the women in our troupe do? We found a makeshift toilet sort of thing, though, but it had no doors, not even a make-do one.

'Who bothers with a door, Sahibji? This is the desert . . . we go behind the dunes and make do. The sand comes in handy. Where in this desert will you find enough water to work a flush?'

'Then where do you get water to bathe and cook?'

'There's a pipeline, Sahibji, but the control is in Jaisalmer. By the time the water reaches here, it is never enough. We order water tankers. The contractors too need to earn a living.'

We reserved a tent for the womenfolk. Water was

available in bottles and we had a plentiful stock of Bisleri.
Our heroine, whom we addressed as Dimpyji, had fired
a gun a number of times in films. But she had never
handled a real gun, never fired real bullets. She asked the
soldier standing in the alcove, 'Is this thing loaded?'

'Yes, certainly madam, it is.'

'May I?'

The soldier jumped down. Dimpyji stepped on the
empty wooden crates by the wall and climbed onto the
alcove. The desert sprawled out like a beautiful, delicate
silken sheet over the earth. Not far away, towards the
right, two palm trees stood tall in their green plumage.
A few thatched houses huddled around them.

'Who lives in those houses?' Dimpyji asked.

'Shepherds, mostly.'

'Is that a village?'

'Yes, something like it.'

'What's its name?'

The soldier had no idea. He looked embarrassed and
began to look sideways. A number of soldiers had come
and stood behind Dimpyji, crowding the door. They
were all trying hard to suppress their smiles. A senior
soldier finally said, 'The village does not have a name.
People call it Pochina Ki Poonchh, the tail of Pochina.'

Laughter crackled through like a piece of chalk
scratching a line on the blackboard. Dimpyji asked the
senior, 'May I fire this gun?'

He hesitated a little before saying, 'Yes, go ahead.'

'But what if somebody from the other side of the border
fires back?'

'Not a problem ji. We normally fire a shot to greet each other.'

'Is that so? And what if I were to fire two shots?'

A smile stayed glued on each and every face.

'Oh . . . that would be a signal to the men on the other side that we are sending people across the border . . . if they want to send somebody across they too fire twice.'

They all broke into laughter but the laughter never left their lips, it stayed glued to their faces. Dimpyji fired a greeting at the enemy outpost. The sound reverberated in the desolate arid desert and began to swim across the border. Gopi Advani was standing next to me. Suddenly he trembled. His lips quivered and tears welled up in his eyes.

'What's the matter with you?' I asked.

'Nothing!' he said in a choked voice. 'Over there on the other side is Sindh . . . my village.' And he walked away.

People in our unit would tease Gopi; they called him Baby Gopi. He was a very emotional man. Tears would well up in his eyes if he were to talk about his mother. His family had stayed back in Sindh after Partition. He had gone to school there for a few years. But with the arrival of the Indian *muhajirs*—the Muslims from India who were forced to go to Pakistan after Partition—life for them became increasingly difficult and they had to leave. That day, seeing Sindh so close, his heart trembled.

I did not see him again that day. He did not even return to the tent at nightfall. When the director inquired about him, I covered for him, 'He's not feeling well. I asked him, to rest in the tent.' But I had begun to worry about Gopi. What if he had scrambled across the border? He wasn't to be found the next morning either, but he resurfaced in the afternoon the day after. I learnt that he indeed had gone over to the other side. But soon he had found himself totally lost.

'Deep in the desert, you tend to lose your orientation. Dunes upon dunes of sand, they all look the same. You climb a dune but the one in front looks the same as the one you just left behind. There was only one thing to do—to retrace my footsteps and head back. But when I turned back the footprints were all gone. To tell you the truth, I was really scared. If it wasn't for Salman, I would be . . . he was godsent.'

'Who's Salman?'

'Let me finish . . . I will tell you. When the desert begins to heat up it really seems as if it is getting angry at you . . . as if it is trying to say "why are you trying to step on my bed". . . pick your feet up, go away. The desert is so vast and I am so puny. I took off my shirt and tied it around my head. A while later I heard the strains of a song. Somebody was singing *maand*. Not very far away. I could make out the song—*Padharo mere desh*—but I could not see anybody. I untied my shirt and began to wave it. God knows how he spotted me or from where because when my eyes fell on him he was on the top of the dune under which I was standing. He was sitting astride a camel; he hollered at me, "*Kotha piyu inchay, Sai?*"

'I don't know how to say it, man, but in that frame of mind, to hear him speak Sindhi it felt as if I was in my mother's arms, as if Mother herself had come to pick me up. He asked me again, "Where are you coming from?" I said, "Pochina." He pulled me up on the back of his camel and spurred the animal into a run.'

'Where did you two go then? Sindh?' I asked.

'No, only up to Miyan Jalaadh, a village behind Pochina. That is where Salman lives.'

'But which side is he from? This side or the other side?'

Gopi told me that Salman was a fugitive from the other side: a murderer on the run. He had killed an admirer of the woman he loved and had run across the border and sought refuge in Miyan Jalaadh. A woman took him in and gave him shelter. He stayed with her for three years and then married her. Now he had two strapping kids with her.

'He never went back to the other side?'

'He does, sometimes, to meet his beloved. The same girl. Now even she is married and all. She, too, has two kids.'

Gopi paused awhile and then resumed his tale, 'When I told him that I too am from the other side, he got all fired up and said, "Come, I will take you to your village." I felt so much like saying yes. I asked him, "Now? In the night?" He looked at me and harrumphed, "O, Sai . . . I may forget the way but my camel will not. Once she starts running she will only stop at her door."

'"Whose?" I asked.

'But it was his wife who answered, "The woman's, who else's? He's got a woman there too. Across the border."

'I looked at her and asked, "And you don't feel bad about it?"

'"I have been telling him, bring her over too . . . the two of us will learn to live together."'

What a wonderful border ours was. When we read about it in our newspapers it seems nothing less than an incendiary line drawn of fire, spewing fire and spouting blood.

The next day, the hero of our film, Banneyji, said to me, 'Yaar, rum won't do. Can't you arrange for some whiskey . . . even Indian whiskey will do.'

We had heard that Indian whiskey got smuggled across the border near a village not far from Pochina. Whiskey got ferried from the Indian side and silver from the Pakistani side. The police from both sides met every month in the village to work out the logistics. A lot of things got ironed out in such meetings: how many sheep strayed from this side, how many camels got caught on the other side, etc.—these meetings took everything into account. The two sides sorted out everything amicably between themselves. On some evenings the Indian side even threw a party in honour of the guests from across the border, opened a few bottles of good whiskey, roasted a few skewers of lamb.

That evening Gopi and I were sitting on one such border outpost, next to Havildar Bujharat Singh. He had just finished giving his advice on how to break in a camel over his wireless radio. He had even ordered for our whiskey bottles over the wireless. Now he was talking to us about the letter that his wife had written him.

'She is a complete idiot, Sahibji . . . she has gone mad . . . she writes anything she feels like. Now you tell me Sahibji . . . what should I do? Shall I protect Hindustan or shall I go and fight the thakur who has usurped her two-finger-width worth of land? Look, Sahibji . . . the entire border is open . . . the enemy can march over at any time. The government has produced bloody nuclear bombs . . . but what has it done for us . . . now even matches are one rupee a box.'

He tried to puff on his beedi but it had gone out on him. He plucked a dried twig from the weave of his charpoy and poked it through the tiny opening in the lantern's housing. The dried twig immediately flared up. He relit his beedi on the flaming twig. He had hardly taken two or three puffs before the beedi once again died on him.

Gopi had pulled out his lighter to light his cigarette. He looked at Gopi and laughed, 'Only if I had a lighter of my own . . . life then would be such fun . . . now you cannot light a beedi with a nuclear bomb, can you? Over!'

The Rams

Suchitgarh is a small hamlet on this side, in Hindustan. Sialkot is a big town on that side—in Pakistan.

Captain Shaheen was a handsome army man in New York. He ran a restaurant named Kashmir. His office was styled like a glorified bunker: the roof replete with artificial leaves sticking out of plastic nets, a number of army caps hung on one wall, military boots carelessly placed upon the floor, a military uniform hung on a clothes hook.

Amjad Islam had invited me over to the restaurant for lunch—and Vakil Ansari escorted me to the place. He was from that side, but he kept inviting all the Urdu poets and writers from this side to his place and in this way indulged his love for the language.

Vakil Ansari had celebrated *Jashn-e-Gopichand Narang* all over the country. He owned a hotel and that was his means of livelihood. Sardar Jafri from this side and

Ahmad Faraz from the other side often stayed as his guests in his house. His favourite phrase was: 'Life's become as commonplace as partridges and quails.' Or another variant of the same: 'Life has reduced us to partridges and quails.' It was a very original phrase, one that I had not come across before—neither on this side nor on the other.

While inviting me over to Captain Shaheen's restaurant, Amjad bhai had said, 'If you want to dine on Eastern cuisine, then you will not find a better place than Shaheen's in the whole of New York.' Amjad bhai was very cautious with the words he picked—he did not call it Indian or Pakistani cuisine. For that matter he did not even refer to it as Punjabi cuisine. He called it 'Eastern'. And he went out of the way to avoid the word Kashmir. But Captain Shaheen was your typical large-hearted army man and he laughed off Amjad bhai's cautionary approach. 'Aji . . . both sides stake their claims on Kashmir—and that's the reason why this restaurant of mine is flourishing,' he said.

Something had upset him in the army and in a sulk he had resigned his commission. 'If I had stayed for just one more month I would have retired as a Major,' he said, 'but somehow, I like the sound of Captain Shaheen better.'

He had participated in the 1971 Indo–Pak war. 'All the action took place on the eastern front, in Bengal. We only had a few skirmishes in Punjab,' he said. He was embroiled in action in one of the battles in the Sialkot sector.

I asked him, 'What is that emotion that makes a soldier out of a man?'

He had grown a thin beard and was in the habit of twirling his moustache as he spoke. 'O ji, that's just a grandiloquent feeling. It is all about the splendour of the uniform and the charm of the army beret, and the status that it adds to a man's prestige. I don't think that men become soldiers to die and kill for the country.' He then burst into laughter, 'Our feud is no war. The wars between Hindustan and Pakistan! Come off it. They keep fighting like schoolchildren—twist this one's arm, break that one's knee, spill some ink over this one's shirt, drive the nib of the pen into that one's side. Remember when we were kids, how we would go to watch sheep ram their horns into each other—you too must have bunked school to see them fight . . .'

I found him a very down-to-earth person. There was a deeply felt honesty in his way of speaking. I must have asked him something that made him say, 'Yes, of course! A soldier too is scared—at first. But after he fires his gun a few times, empties a few bullets, fear takes flight. When bullets are fired, there's a kind of smell that permeates the air—that of burnt gunpowder. And at the front, you get intoxicated with it, sort of addicted to it. When the guns fall silent and the trance is about to be broken you begin to fire again. Not necessarily at the enemy. Just so that you do not sober up.'

He paused and then added, 'When you face your fear, you become familiar with it and familiarity makes it lose its meaning, loosen its grip—fear ceases to be fear.'

To me it seemed as if he was asking people at the front to get intimate with death—it will come when it comes.

He said, 'Right in the beginning, at the outset of your training when you are prostrate on the ground, grazing your knees and your elbows, the thought does come time and again to quit, to give it all up. But when your bargedar (brigadier) singles you out and reprimands you on your mistake, when he screams at you, demanding to know which part of the country you are from, then believe me, sahib, you are unable to take the name of your village or state—it is just so embarrassing.'

Perhaps this is what translates into honour for a soldier—the honour of the soil that you come from, the honour that a soldier needs to defend at all costs.

Captain Shaheen kept up his narration. 'Suchitgarh is a small little hamlet—of a few houses. Some had already been abandoned because they were very close to the border and some when we marched into the village. It was necessary for us to inspect each and every house: when you win a territory without any resistance, you are wise to suspect an enemy manoeuvre. It could be one of their traps.'

He was of the opinion that there is a great difference in the temperament of the soldiers on the two sides. 'They are both Punjabis but the soldiers on this side—they are a little more aggressive. And those on the other side—they are of a more pacific nature, more calm. Farmers on the other side till their lands within inches of the border. But on this side, they let at least two–three hundred yards of barren land distance their houses and farms from the border. In such places, troops of five to seven soldiers patrol the borders on either side. And often they are in such close proximity to each other that they can light each other's cigarettes.

'The soldiers on this side are commonly Punjabis but on the other side you often find non-Punjabis. Many a times, the soldiers on this side shout across the border, "So, bhai! Where from?" If that soldier is from down south he shouts back in English but normally what you hear is Hindi laced with Urdu.

'After seizing Suchitgarh, I took a troop of four or five soldiers and started checking the houses in the village. As my men pushed open the door of a house, they found a small boy cowering in one corner of the house, scared out of his wits. My men called out to me, "Sirji."

'The moment I reached there the boy leapt towards me and hugged me. He just wouldn't let go. My men pulled him away, somehow. I was troubled; what was I to do with him? I could hardly get a word out of the boy—he was too scared to even tell me the name of his parents. He just stood there, shaking in fear. I told him to scamper, to run away. But he just couldn't. So I put him in my jeep and brought him back to my post. I gave him something to eat and asked him to lie down in a corner. I instructed my men not to let a word of this out—technically, he was our prisoner of war. I was duty-bound to report this matter to my headquarters and throw him into a jail along with other prisoners. But there was something in his eyes, his innocence perhaps, that made me wish the poor boy well.

'After noon the next day, I took out my badge-shadge and went on a patrol to the same border village. On a farm a little away from the village I found an old Sikh rinsing his mouth at the tubewell. I shouted, "Sardarji . . . oye . . . come here!" He looked in my direction and I gestured to him to come over. When he came near me, wiping his hands on the tail end of his turban, I asked him, "You haven't gone?"

'He looked at me, a little taken aback, "Where?"

'"Everybody else has gone. Left the village. Why haven't you?"

'"Lai . . . I have already left my village on the other side with you," he said pointing across the border with both his hands. "What have you come here for now . . . to grab my fields?"

'The Sikh seemed to be in a rage. I tried to pacify him and said, "A kid from Suchitgarh . . . about seven or eight years old . . . has strolled over to our side. I believe his parents have left the village."

'"So?"

'"If I bring him over, will you take him to his parents?"

'The sardar fell in deep thought. After a long pause he nodded, "All right."

'I asked him to come back at five in the evening. Never till then had I seen a smile glint off such yellowed, decaying teeth. The old Sikh laughed, "Let the boy off. Imprison me instead. Take me with you. My village is over on that side. A little further down from Sialkot. Chajra." He sounded ecstatic—drunk just on the name of his village.

'I could not make it back to the village that evening. Our commander was paying us a visit. And it took all our efforts to keep the boy hidden from him. We fed him and then hoisted him on to the loft of the control room. When the commander wanted to inspect the control room, we pulled him down from the loft and bundled him behind the gunny sacks of the storeroom and then later quickly locked him in the latrine behind the barracks. It was totally illegal to keep him with us. Heads would roll if the commander were to get a whiff of him. There was a moment when I was on the verge of ordering my soldiers to tie him in a gunny sack and dump him in the old Sikh's field. A sword kept dangling over our heads all through the commander's stay.

'News from the eastern front, from Bengal, had begun to pour in. And it depressed the hell out of us. The Indian armed forces were with the Mukti Bahini and Yahya Khan . . . well . . . leave that be.'

There was a long pause. Captain Shaheen's eyes had begun to soften, I could discern a hint of hurt pride in them. His face was criss-crossed with emotions. Finally, he spoke again.

'The next day too there was a lot of troop movement. The day whittled away. The sun was about to set when I reached the border along with the kid. I was surprised to see the old Sikh still waiting there. There was a small troop of four or five soldiers with him. One of them stepped forward and addressed me, "Captain or Major?" Soldiers do not wear their ranks in ribbons at the front, but still it is not difficult to make out an officer amongst the ranks. The soldier who spoke was also either a Captain or a Major. I stepped forward, shook his hand and handed the boy over to him. "He's from Suchitgarh. We found him hiding in one of the village houses," I said.

'"So . . . where are you from . . . who are your parents?" the officer asked him, a little sternly.

'The boy shuddered once again. He raised his eyes in my direction and said, "Chacha . . . I am not from this side . . . I am from the other side," he gestured in our direction, towards our side, "from Chajra, a little further down from Sialkot."

'We were all stunned. I looked at the old Sikh. A smile once again glinted off his yellowed teeth. He moved towards the boy, ruffled his hair with the fondness reserved for one's own and with tears that refused to stay within his eyes asked, "Really? You are from Chajra?"

'I yelled at him, "Then what the hell were you doing here?"

'Tears began to roll down his checks. "I had run away from school . . . to . . . to . . . see the ram fight."'

Captain Shaheen looked into my eyes and said earnestly, 'Believe me, Sahib, the two of us, soldiers both, were standing before that seven–eight-year-old like two idiotic schoolmasters. And our faces looked like those of rams.'

IV

A legion of heads, a throng of limbs
Abandoned apparatus from a defunct factory
Spare parts all—

Hilsa

Vibhuti dawdled through the house, rearranging the folds of his dhoti, and stopped at the kitchen door. 'The newspaper hasn't arrived yet, has it?' he sighed. 'Now it seems Bagbazaar Road too has been blockaded.'

But his sigh was lost on Kanchan. She was too engrossed in the fish that she was dressing. 'Look at its eyes—beautiful, aren't they? Mesmerizing like a mermaid's.' She scooped up a mug of water, poured it into the flat-bottomed pan and began to bathe the fish in it.

A hint of mischief stretched across Vibhuti's lips, 'Enamoured with these unseasonal showers, seems like Ramu found you some mangoes in December . . . eh?'

'How do you mean?'

An impish glee lit up Vibhuti's eyes, 'It's summer now. You shouldn't eat fish in the months that do not have the letter R in them. It's prohibited!' Now that he had Kanchan's undivided attention he elaborated, 'Like in the months of May, June, July, August . . . come to think of it, all the other months, September through April, they all have the letter R in them.'

Kanchan spelled out the months in her mind and looked at her husband, impressed. 'Yes, it's as you say . . . but why is it forbidden to eat fish in these months?'

Like a typical Bengali husband, Vibhuti stuffed a pinch of snuff up each nostril, rearranged the folds of his dhoti once again and sat down on the threshold of the kitchen. 'Those are the months in which the fish breed . . . they are pregnant . . . and just like when the wife is pregnant it is forbidden to have . . .'

'Dhat! What are you saying . . .' she blushed, 'you have grown old but the devil still has you in his clutch . . . go, go . . . off you go!' She pushed Vibhuti away from the kitchen.

Laughing, Vibhuti sauntered into the living room and fidgeted with the TV controls. The television was rife with news of the riots. The rioters were on a rampage. The markets were all closed. The local administration had clamped a curfew in many places.

'Perhaps this is why,' Vibhuti muttered under his breath, 'the fishermen could not bring their haul to the markets and Ramu found a cheap deal at the ghat.'

He ambled over to the kitchen to impress his wife once again with his power of deduction, but Kanchan was not there. He heard the sound of gurgling water and deduced that the wife must have gone for her bath at the hand-pump. He crossed the kitchen and could see that Kanchan had spread her sari on the clothesline to carve herself a private bathing space.

'Are you listening?'

'Yes, tell me?' her voice seemed wet, coming from behind sheets of falling water.

'Our Ramu . . . you know . . . he must have gone to the ghat early in the morning . . .' He lifted the improvised screen a little.

'Dhat!' A volley of water hit Vibhuti's face. 'Out . . . out you go . . . thank God, this shameless man has an office to go to on most days.'

Vibhuti laughed and began to wipe his face on his wife's sari. 'It's not my fault that the newspaper hasn't arrived . . . what's an idle man to do? Shall I dress the fish?'

'No! Don't you dare step into my kitchen!'

Poor Vibhuti! He had too much time on his hands. Aimlessly he drifted through the house. There wasn't much on the television to hold his attention. *Chitra Geet* and then the news and then *Chitra-Geet* all over again. He couldn't relish the song videos on the black-and-white TV. God! In this day and age of colour, a black-and-white TV! The clothes and the skin of the gyrating sirens in the same shade! Imagine having no idea where the heroine's blouse ended and where her skin began! This was certainly not done.

He heard the sound of Ramu's voice somewhere in the house. God alone knew when he was in the house, and when he was out. It seemed like he worked for the entire neighbourhood. Ramu was standing outside Kanchan's improvised bathroom, asking her, 'Bouma, shall I grind the masala for the fish? Are you planning to cook it with mustard?'

'Go, get the masala ground in Tuntuni's grinder . . . I shall be done with my chores by then,' he heard Kanchan say.

Tuntuni was the youngest daughter of his next-door neighbour. He heard Ramu's retreating footsteps and the sound of the gate closing. Vibhuti did not like Ramu talking to his wife while she was having a bath. And now there was nothing but static on the TV. He turned the TV off and plopped on the easy chair.

When he heard the ringing of the prayer bells he realized that Kanchan was dressed and in the puja room. Soon she would be here with the bowl of prasad in her hand and when he would stretch out his open palms towards her, her eyebrows would arch and she would say go wash your hands first and lazily he would tilt his head back and open his mouth and Kanchan would drop the prasad into his mouth.

And that was what happened. The moment Kanchan stepped into the room she shot at him, 'What? You haven't had your bath yet?'

'Un-hoon!' He shook his head and opened his mouth. Kanchan dropped the prasad into his mouth and in doing so her still-wet hair fell on his face and while brushing her hair off his face he playfully squeezed her cheeks.

'Uff! You men . . . you have no sense of propriety . . . this isn't a proper time to . . .'

'Must I fix a time to appreciate beauty?'

'Liar!' She hurried away.

Vibhuti could detect a blush on her face and tremor in her voice as she spun away from him. He smiled to himself.

Now he once again found himself with a lot of time on his hands. With nothing to do, he went and stood at his window and peeped into the lives of his neighbours. A crow flew in with a piece of raw mutton in its beak and perched on the wall separating his house from that of his neighbour's. Another crow flew in and lowered itself onto the other end of the wall. When it started to hop closer, the crow with the piece of mutton in its beak flapped its wings and flew away. The other crow flew away too. Vibhuti moved away from the window and soon found himself once again in the kitchen.

The hilsa was still lying in the flat-bottomed pan, its mouth a little agape as if it was trying to say something. And those wide-open eyes, weren't they mesmerizing, beautiful!

Kanchan reached for the fish-knife, fixed it between her toes and picked the hilsa out of the pan. She ran her hand over its slithery body to wipe off any stray drops of water that still clung on to it and then in one smooth stroke chopped it into three neat pieces: first she severed the head, then lopped off the tail and in the end split the truncated body wide down the middle. The water in the pan turned a deep red.

'You were right,' she looked at her husband. 'The hilsa was pregnant. Look at this . . . it is stuffed with roe.'

'Very lucky,' Vibhuti smiled, and began to polish his spectacles. 'Fry them separately . . . hilsa roe is a delicacy.'

It was precisely at that moment that he heard the short punch of the doorbell, the thud of a falling newspaper, and the delivery man yelling as he pushed his cycle away, 'Paper, babu!'

Vibhuti got up and fetched the newspaper. The front page screamed out a big bold headline about the riots that had engulfed the city. There were a few photographs too. One photograph was of a girl. She had been pregnant; she had been gang-raped; and she had bled to death. In the photograph her mouth was slightly open, as if she was trying to say something. And her eyes were wide open. Her eyes looked like those of the hilsa in the pan.

The Stone Age

The bomb did not fall anywhere near the house, but still, the walls could not withstand the impact of the explosion. Mud walls—what could you expect of them? They shook, began to crumble, and within moments were reduced to nothing more than a heap of rubble. Nasir's younger sister got entrapped in its dusty entrails—and that was the end of her. The elder one snatched him up in her arms and ran. They ran for their lives, ran outdoors without a veil. A gossamer of dust from the crumbling debris had veiled the streets. Nasir's father grabbed his mother's hand, scooped the bundle off the floor and darted out. They had bundled everything they owned in a small little fold of canvas and kept it ready for such occasions.

Nasir was all of four then.

'Abbu . . . this way Abbu . . . the firangis are on that side.' He jumped off his sister's lap, guiding them. He was blessed with far-sightedness. A jeep full of soldiers sped by, showering bullets. 'Nasir saved us! Nasir saved our lives!' His sister smothered him with kisses. His mother blessed him, praying for his share of misfortunes to fall in her lot.

Nasir's eyes shone with a strange brilliance. He had by now begun to get used to the life of the jungle; he had begun to forget what his own home looked like. They would wander for 2–3 months at a stretch and then return home, back to the pots and pans—a sort of return to civilization. They would take care of things, pick up the old threads of life, and then, once again, flee a few months later. There was a grandmother—all she would do was lie in the corner of the house like a sack full of straw.

Nasir was only two years old when he first heard the roar of a plane and then the accompanying, earth-shattering sound of exploding bombs. His ears had begun to ache—his eardrums nearly split. The entire house had begun to shake and he was shivering, clinging to the bosom of his mother. His mother had him wrapped around her chest with a thick piece of cloth. The bundle with all their worldly possessions was in one of her hands and with the other she held on to Bano, his younger sister. His father clutched a small attaché case under his armpit. His lips were quivering in silent prayer. He had dragged his mother to the door and said, 'Amma, just try . . . just do it. Take Allah's hand in yours and let's go . . . to the masjid.'

God knew who his grandmother was cursing—his father or Allah. There was a sparkle in Nasir's eyes even then. He had seen stars being plucked out of the sky and he had seen numerous suns exploding on the ground. An innocent question had arisen in his heart then: 'Why is Allah so scary, so dreadful? Why does he keep terrorizing us?'

Two years was hardly any time to understand the goings-on about you. But the eyes, they took in more than they could digest, to regurgitate and chew on things at a later age—like a camel.

The masjid was reeking of blood. Severed hands, torn shoulders, bleeding necks—there were more men bleeding than ones unharmed. But for Nasir this was normal. Where Nasir was born, blood would rain more often than water from the skies. He would jump into a puddle of blood and splash his feet in it the way other kids jumped into puddles of rainwater.

New sounds, new names fell upon his ears at the masjid. He was familiar with names of people from his tribe. But names like Russia, America, Bush, Traganoff, Greganoff, Firangi, Copter—they must have been names of people from another tribe. People living in another jungle—beyond those hills perhaps, from where all those flying machines would fly out, over which he could see the flying machines hovering, from where cannonballs of fire would shoot out at them . . . to wreak havoc in their lives, to break down their walls. He could never forget the sight of the walls falling on his younger sister. She was too young to even know how to scream.

'Houses crumble, Abbu—then why do we live in houses?' He was three years old when he had asked his father this question. In those days they were refugees in a city of concrete roofs.

'Because outside it is raining fire, bombs are falling!' his father had said.

'Who drops them?'

'They . . . those firangis . . . those who fly about in helicopters.'

'Why do they drop bombs?'

'Because they are our enemies.'

'Are we their enemies too?'

'Of course we are!'

About a year and a half after that last question, he asked, 'So can't we too drop bombs on their hills?'

'But son, we don't have any helicopters!'

'Then how?'

'We have got fidayeens, don't we? This is why we send fidayeen!'

This was beyond Nasir's comprehension. But he was learning. He made another deposit in his piggy bank—the word fidayeen. He would come back to it when he grew up a little more. He would fall silent but he would never be satisfied with his father's answers. These questions would keep hovering like bees over his head. So he would go out and begin to work on his catapult.

Nasir would remember his grandmother often. The few months that they had spent in the Aabnoosi Masjid in Kandahar, she had narrated to him a number of stories.

'A horrifically tall devil kidnapped the fairy and imprisoned her in the twin towers in the sky,' one story went. 'He imprisoned the fairy in one tower and he himself lived in the other. He had clipped the wings of the fairy so that she could not even fly away from there. And the towers were so tall that no human could ever scale them. Whenever a crowd at the base of the towers would become unruly the devil would pluck a feather off the fairy's back and flick it down toward the crowd. And the crowd would run amuck to catch the feather, wild in ecstasy, and cover a distance of thousands of kilometres trying to grab the feather.'

'Even the prince?'

'No! But what could a lone prince do? He could neither scale those towers nor could he fly . . .'

Suddenly, the coin popped out of his piggy bank and he made a withdrawal against the deposit he had made long ago—the word came to his mind. 'Fidayeen,' he said to himself. 'Why did he not send in the fidayeens?'

He had finally grasped the meaning of the word. If his grandmother was here with him, he would have told her. He asked his father and he said, 'Allah called her. She's gone to be with him!'

'Dadi too!' And then he fell silent.

God knew whether the minarets of the masjid were growing smaller or if it was he who was growing taller. He would squeeze himself out of his grandmother's bundle and run up the stairs of the minarets like a rat running out of a sack full of grain. From the balcony of the minarets, he could see the entire city. From his vantage point, the city looked like a huge brick kiln—smoke snaking its way up from places at regular intervals. He took them to be the eateries—they must have been roasting mutton, they must have been skewering kebabs.

Nasir was growing up fast. His legs peeked out of his salwar, the sleeves of his shirt rode high on his arms. He would look at his grandmother accusingly as if she had filched the clothes from the neighbour's clothesline. Once, perched on that very minaret, he heard the rumbling of the tanks. When they drove past the bazaar the entire ground quaked. He could feel the ground quiver even from atop the minaret. Must be those humungous mythical, evil rhinoceroses his grandmother's fantasy stories were filled with, he thought, stumping through the earth with their snouts in the air—to spit out fire.

And then there was another attack. The masjid was surrounded by those mythical, evil rhinoceroses. And they kept up their siege for quite a few days. Every night a few men would be herded out like cattle into the night. Like sheep and goats, on all fours, on their knees and elbows, they would go crawling, creeping, slithering through the lanes and escape to freedom across the maidan. Nasir managed to escape, too, along with his elder sister and mother. His father and grandmother had to stay still at the basement of the masjid.

There was another village behind the hills—a village of mud houses. A few families took refuge there in a cowshed. The place was relatively silent—you hardly heard people here. Nasir's father would periodically come, spend a few nights with them and then go back. And then once, he did not return. Nasir's mother would often fall on her knees in supplication, trying to appease

Allah, beseech him for his blessings, ask him for his indulgence to keep her family safe. Her eyes would be brimming with tears all the time. Nasir would lie on the floor watching his mother. He asked her once, 'What blessings were you asking from Allah?'

'I was asking Allah to keep your father safe, son!'

Nasir kept lying there, kept looking at the vast expanse of the sky, and then softly asked, 'Ammi, on which side is Allah on? Ours or theirs?'

When he turned to look, his mother was long gone.

One night, Nasir tucked his catapult into the folds of his salwar and groped his way back into the basement of the masjid through the labyrinth of tunnels. The scene that befell his eyes inside the masjid shook him to the core. He fell in a heap there itself. The entire masjid was in ruins. It was filled with rubble and when his eyes got accustomed to the darkness he could see the hands and feet of the dead people jutting out of the debris. When day broke, he began to move towards the main door. Then he saw a few men. They had wound their turbans around their noses and mouths. They had shovels and spades in their hands. Perhaps they had come to clean the debris. Nasir hid himself from them without being caught. When he came out he saw a cordon of people outside and he jumped into a truck parked against the wall.

And then Nasir could feel halves and quarters of bodies and severed body parts raining down on him. He remained huddled in one corner of the truck under the human debris, afraid to move, afraid he would get caught. The sight was not all that unfamiliar. Half-torn,

severed halves of carcasses, half-skinned, half-peeled
bodies of animals he had seen arrive by the cartload at
the local butcher's. He stayed huddled in the corner of
the truck. The truck began to move. God alone knew the
shop of the butcher at which they would dump these
bodies. Over the drive of a few hours that followed, Nasir
either fell unconscious or fell asleep; he woke up when
the truck emptied its load on a hill.

He rolled down the slope; his fall broke only when he
hit the bottom of the hill with a thud, and his eyes were
forced open. He had fallen next to a huge pit that had been
dug at the foot of the hill. The truck was returning after
dumping its rubbish. The huge cliff stretched its head out
in all its bald glory. Indomitable, the mountaintop reared
its naked pate. He crawled out from under the inhuman
remains of human lives. And like a scared vixen running
for its life, he crawled up the slopes of the hill on all fours.
Craters were open along the slope like mole-holes. He
took refuge in a crater-like cave.

From the top of the hill, it looked like a dumping yard.
By evening the pit was full to its brim and they closed its
mouth. That night Nasir slept in the cave. In the darkness
of the night, he could hear some human voices slithering
across the silent, sultry air. Perhaps there were people
who lived in the adjoining caves. And then he saw a
number of eyes glistening in the dark—wild rabbits
perhaps. Nasir groped for stones. The catapult was still
in the folds of his salwar; he pulled it out. He picked a
sharp stone by touch and began to sharpen it against a
bigger stone.

One of his grandmother's stories came to his mind: 'In the beginning, humans carved stones into weapons. They would live in caves and hunt. Some tribes had fire. They were *afzal*, the blessed ones! They left the jungles and started to live in the plains. And they would travel huge distances and conquer foreign lands.'

Nasir was grinding the smaller stone against the bigger one and was making himself a lethal weapon of stone.

The Search

They forced me to open my suitcase and went through its entire contents. I could understand their rummaging through my belongings. But when the male soldiers picked out the bras and probed them with lingering fingers, anger shot up my spine. What on earth could be hidden under a bra—grenades? Now, come on, I wouldn't be smuggling grenades in the cups of those bras. I couldn't contain myself when they picked up my lipsticks and began to inspect them closely. And when they started to take apart my lipstick cases, I lost it. 'These are not bullets. They are lipsticks. Keep them. Load them if you can in your rifles! And shoot with them for all I care!' I said.

Shameless, he bared his ugly, yellowing teeth and said, 'Gone are those days of the double-barrelled shotguns, madam. Now we clip hundred-cartridge magazines into our rifles.' Perhaps the woman constable with him understood my sarcasm. She tried to explain, 'We have to be extra-cautious on the Srinagar flights, madam. Come, come this way!' And she invited me to step into a half-open curtained enclosure for a through body search.

I was going to Kashmir in search of my roots: to look at my beginnings. However I am not Kashmiri. I just know this much: that my father and mother had gone to Kashmir and when they came back I had already taken root in my mother's womb. 'On those icy cold waters of the Jhelum, in a floating houseboat, atop a delicately carved walnut wood bed, when two pious souls were giving birth to a sacred moment . . .' Mom would read out in a poetic style her entries from her Kashmir journal, relishing every single syllable, every single memory that her tongue could wrap itself around. She would regale me with stories of Dad in Kashmir.

'He just didn't know how to ride a horse. A stool would be placed next to the horse. Your father would first climb up on the stool and then the groom would coax the horse near the stool, and then and only then would your dad be able to get astride the horse. Even then, five times out of ten, he would fall on his face.'

Dad would peep out from behind the newspaper he was reading and interject, 'Don't you lie, I fell off only once!'

'Once? And what about the time when Your Highness, the Lord Pantaloon came undone!' Mom was from Lucknow, and Dad from Kolkata.

'Oh . . . now, come on . . . when the legs of the stool cave in, one does fall. It wasn't my fault!'

'Remember that one time when you found yourself atop the groom and not the horse?'

'Now . . . come off it . . . that cranky horse just cantered away . . . just when I had lifted myself off the table. All right now . . . that's enough.' At this point in the conversation, Dad would turn to me, 'Shonali, don't you believe a single word your mother says. When I take you to Kashmir, I will show you how good a rider I am!'

'Kashmir,' Mom would sigh deeply. 'Now that's impossible! Who goes to Kashmir any more? Gone are the days when you could simply pick up your bags and head off to paradise, year after year. Strife's in the air now. Bullets rend its quiet. Flowers no longer bloom there—death does!'

It must have been around 1981–82, or was it 1982–83? I was still studying in school. The news on the radio made my blood boil. Who the hell were these Pakistanis to misappropriate our Kashmir? As if Kashmir was my personal property, my fiefdom.

And then Mom would remember her Kashmir days again and say, 'We had a Kashmiri servant. A young man . . . hardly a man, rather a boy . . . whenever we went to Kashmir, we would hire his services for about a month. His name was Wazir Ali. Sometimes we would stay in a house boat, sometimes at the Oberoi Hotel. At the Oberoi, we would always stay in its annexe. There was a sprawling lawn right in front with two chinar trees: tall, stout, leafy—and majestic. They had a regal bearing—they always looked like royalty to me. An emperor and an empress, hands across their chests, surveying the waters of the Dal Lake, lording over it, and we mere mortals would be allowed only the view of the lawns. They both had pride, I tell you—Emperor Jehangir and Empress Noor Jehan . . .' Mom was indeed a poet but limited herself only to diaries. I brought her back to what she had started talking about, 'You were telling me something about Wazir Ali.'

'Oh yes! Every evening he would take you out for a stroll in your pram. And then one day he did not return. Night fell. It was quite late. We began to worry. And then he went out to look for you.'

'He? Who?'

'Your father. Who else? Mr Arun Banerjee. I kept waiting—restless; worrying myself to death. He returned after what seemed like an age to me. In a taxi—you, your pram, your father and he. I mean not Wazira, but another Kashmiri. I asked your father, "Where's Wazira?" He looked at me in a hurt sort of way. He dropped you in my arms, threw the pram in the veranda and called for the Kashmiri who had come with him. "Moorti Lal!" he shouted and then took out a fifty-rupee note and handed it to him. That Moorti Lal was an incessant talker and he started off, "Sahib, how could you entrust him with such a little kid? Thank God, he headed straight home, what if he had run away with her somewhere else . . .?" Your father dismissed him with a wave of his hand and the man quietly walked away.'

'Fifty rupees! Is that all I was worth?' I butted in, just for kicks.

'Fifty rupees was a princely sum in those days!'

I was still curious about the story, worried where Wazira had taken me.

'He took you to his house, to flaunt you to his grandmother. Wazira was an orphan. His parents had been trapped in a snowy avalanche—they were never found. Not even their dead bodies. Wazira had to stay many a night in the hotel on night duty. And whenever he returned home in the mornings, his grandmother would get after him, she would hurl a thousand angry questions and insults at him. He would try to pacify his grandmother by saying that he had got married and had spent the night with his wife. And that he even had a little daughter with her. And because of his grandmother's horrible mood swings he was scared to bring her home.'

I was beginning to like Wazira, albeit just in the quiet of my heart. He had that quaintness, like the heroes in fairytales that grandma told you. His story too seemed like a fairytale to me, then. And it seems like a fairytale even now. I felt that fairytales were born in Kashmir and they trickled downwards to the plains only to avoid the icy Kashmiri winter. Sometimes it occurred to me that had Wazira really ran away with me, I would have grown up in Kashmir. But I did not cherish the idea of separating from my folks in the story.

'Did Wazira ever come back?' I asked.

'Yes, he did. He begged our forgiveness and apologized

profusely. We hired him all over again but we never ever again let him take you out for a stroll.'

I found an album in the house. It was filled with old photographs, but Wazira was not to be found in a single one of them. I found photographs of mine clicked in Gulmarg, Yusmarg, Pahalgam and Chandanwadi— nothing less than illustrations from old books of fairytales.

It was only when I was reading philosophy in college that I asked Mom, 'Shall I go visit Kashmir in these holidays?'

'Don't you see the news on TV? These Kashmiris have wreaked havoc . . .'

I was still in college when I saw it on TV—there was some cricket match being played and Kashmiri youths were shouting anti-India slogans. There were also a number of turbaned Sikh youths in the sloganeering crowd.

And then an incident happened—the terrorists abducted the daughter of a Kashmiri minister. I was about to blurt out that he must have taken her to meet his grandmother but just stopped short—Dad was furious. He was pacing up and down the room and he suddenly turned and roared, 'They are making deals with the terrorists. They are exchanging the minister's daughter for captured terrorists. What on earth do they think they are doing? Would they have agreed to this exchange if the kidnapped woman was an ordinary man's daughter? Would they? You could have gone and yelled into their ears but they would not have registered a single word. All they would have done is issue statements: "These are disturbed times". Have they forgotten what happened during Partition? What they did to us during Partition? Treaties are being signed. Deals are being made with the terrorists!'

Mom asked, 'Then why don't they confront Pakistan? They are the ones that are pulling the strings of these terrorists. They are the ones who are doing this.'

I heard Dad acknowledge for the first time, 'Our people are no less! To hold on to their power these people keep swapping sheepskins.'

I felt bad. God alone knew why—neither Mom nor Dad was from Kashmir, and yet . . .

Somewhere around this time, I saw a Kashmiri youth in Dad's office one day. He was radiant, handsome. He was looking for a job. Dad asked, 'Where are you from?'

The poor guy managed to say in a mousy voice, 'From Kashmir, sir; but I am no rioter; I am no terrorist.'

Dad dismissed him saying, 'Call on me again. Right now, there isn't any vacancy.'

I knew Dad was lying. He simply did not want to entangle himself in officious, mile-long inquiries. Those days the police would keep a sharp eye on all the Kashmiris who had come down to the plains from paradise. Forget Kashmiris, if people so much as heard you say that you were a Muslim, there went your ability to get a job or even rent a place.

Once when Dad was in the hospital, recuperating, I bumped into Dr Basu, our family physician. After that the talk turned towards my marriage. I was nearly done with my studies: it was my last year at university and I had already started working as a rookie reporter with *Hindustan Times*. When Mom asked when I planned to get married, I quipped, 'I will! Provided he takes me to Kashmir for our honeymoon!'

'Kashmir! No!' Dad dismissed the idea with a wave of his hand. He did not say anything more; not because he did not want to—his doctor had advised him not to exert himself. I looked at Mom and said, 'You were the one who said that the idea of me was conceived there.'

Dad waved his hand in the air and went away. That was the end of the conversation—he died soon after.

And now, after so many years, I was off to trace my roots. My heart was bouncing like a rubber ball inside my ribcage when the plane landed in Srinagar. And the moment I stepped out of the airport, I saw what I had not seen anywhere else in India.

The first thought that came to mind was: Has the war started? Has Pakistan attacked us? There were more Indian soldiers than Kashmiris on the locked-down roads of Srinagar. Everywhere there were tanks, trucks, guns, checkposts; there was a bunker on every road, and platoons of soldiers. The bus that I boarded from the airport to the city was stopped three times. And thrice did gun-toting soldiers step on board, rifling through the passengers' belongings, their gaze piercing us all.

'Whose is this?'

'What's in this?'

Finally they stepped down. The bus trundled ahead.

By now I felt as if my breath was being stifled. When

the bus stopped for the third time, a soldier, before alighting from the bus, looked at me through rapacious eyes and barked in crude Hindi, 'Where the hell are you off to, girl?'

I did not like the way he addressed me. I spoke in English, in a tone full of scorn, reserved in India for talking to social inferiors, 'What do you mean where am I going?'

He grunted 'Hoon' and turned and stepped off. I figured he did not understand English and was too proud to admit it. But nobody else on the bus said anything.

I was looking for a regular place to stay, and I was hoping that I would find something around Dal Lake. If I had money I would have stayed at the annexe in Oberoi, I thought.

The surface of the lake was covered in layers of green mulch and the rotting roots of unwanted weeds. A few houseboats were still afloat, anchored at the shore— frayed, dilapidated, praying for a watery grave in the waters of the lake that they had always called home, rot and decay their only companions.

Time and again, tears would well up in my eyes. And, frustrated, I would wipe them away and curse myself, 'Where on earth is your engraved walnut bed now, eh?' My voice choked on my own tears. I did not hear my normal voice ever again after that.

Nobody was willing to put up a single girl in a lodging house or a hotel. Neither my English nor the *Hindustan Times* identity card in my purse was of any help. And seeking the help of the police or the army would be useless. The moment you were associated with them, the locals were sure not to even look in your direction.

Khalil trotted off in his Kashmiri as he put my luggage in his auto, 'You are alone, memsaab. Kashmiri too scared of Hindoostani fauj. They grab anybody from the street and march off . . .' he paused, 'and that person is never ever seen or heard of again . . . God knows in which jail that man disappears.'

All the pent-up anger inside him was finding vent—firing like the exhaust of his auto. He kept on venting. Perhaps he wanted to burn out all the diesel inside him. 'Nobody is going to keep you in a otel—the army would get an excuse to raid the premises and will grab and take the otel-wallah away. If the otel-wallah is old, they will not take him away. But they will take away either his young son, or young son-in-law, or his young banja, batija . . . any of his young relation will do. They have their sight on the youth of Kashmir. They simply want to wipe the youth of Kashmir away . . .'

His voice was becoming increasingly raspier. Suddenly he stopped his auto at the turn of a lane and looked in my direction, 'What do you people want, enh? What do you want from us? Why don't you just let us be, leave us on our own? Now even our green has turned red . . . the grass growing on our earth has become red . . . enh . . .'

His voice became choked, like mine. I sat there with my palms covering my face. I had never ever felt so ashamed of being a Hindustani.

Khalil picked up my suitcase and entered his aunt's

place. Khalil's aunt, his bua, was a wise old woman, well past her middle years. 'You put up here, sister, with my aunt,' he said. 'I shall come every morning and take you wherever you want to go . . . but you must never venture out alone again.'

He left, wiping his tears with his hands, tending to his pain. God alone knew what sort of memories he was nursing, God alone knew what old wounds had opened up again. He neither asked for money, nor talked about the rent.

But I did not pay heed to his words. I patched up something to tell the aunt and left the house on my own. The house was not far away from Dal Lake. Walking by its shore, I soon found myself in front of the Oberoi Palace. The gates were pulled shut, and barbed wire fenced its boundary as far as I could see. I pulled through the barbed-wire fence and entered the complex. A few roosting birds fluttered their wings, cooed something to each other. A few flapped their way up the trees and perched on the branches. They were very alert. I slowly made my way towards the palace.

From the roof of the main building hung huge sheets of tarpaulin that reached the ground. The hotel was closed to the public. Part of the complex had been taken over by army troops, who had started their army kitchen. The veranda was overridden by mildew. A stench invaded my nostrils; I covered my nose with a handkerchief. The annexe was shut. The lawns were covered with rubble and rubbish. And the two chinars stood with their heads bowed, hands tied—like slaves. There was a pronounced droop in their shoulders. They looked old. I began to feel suffocated.

I returned to Bua with my breath stifled; she fixed me a bed in the mezzanine.

I got up early in the morning with the chirping of children. It was the first time that I had heard a happy sound since my arrival. I got up and threw the window open. It looked onto a graveyard where children were playing hide-and-seek. Amongst old chipped tombstones were numerous fresh graves—the mud on some still seemed moist. Perhaps this was the safest place for the children to play. When I came down Bua was nowhere to be seen. But she had laid out a bucket of water for my bath. A cake of soap and a fresh towel were kept at one side. I was not used to bathing with cold water—but then this wasn't a hotel. I cupped the ice-cold water in my hands and slowly began to rinse myself. I tried to get my body acclimatized to the chilly water slowly; it was pretty cold. Then I began to wash myself. After I had poured a few mugs of water over my body, I got used to it. I only felt cold when I stopped pouring the water over my body. As I kept bathing, slowly, all the pain, all the complaints got washed away.

Bua had a young son, Aziz Ali. He was learning computers, till the police came and hauled him away from the shop. It was rumoured that he had met up with some Pakistani—it was the Pakistani who had given him away. Nine years had passed and still there was no news of him. Whenever someone was killed in a police encounter, Bua would go and have a look—sometimes at police stations,

sometimes at the morgue. Whichever jail she could get
the address of, she would go looking there for her son.
She had been to all the jails in Kashmir. Her hand still
hovered over the flame of hope; she kept burning; she
refused to believe the worst. Her tears had all dried up
but she still kept crying. I told her, 'Bua, maybe he's gone
over to Pakistan, or maybe he's in Tihar Jail.'

'Where's that?'

'In Delhi.'

Her face turned ashen. But I could not bring myself
to tell her that maybe he was not alive any more, maybe
he was dead.

One day, much before daybreak, the police cordoned
off the entire area. Military trucks parked on all four sides.
Searchlights were sprung atop two trucks. A megaphone
boomed. People were ordered to get out of their houses
and assemble in the graveyard. The military was to
search all the houses. People hurried out of their houses
within minutes, as if they had rehearsed for this event a
number of times. The sun came out and climbed halfway
across the sky. Hungry and thirsty, people stayed put
in the graveyard for hours without protest, without any
complaints. The search of their houses continued.

At midday, I gathered some courage and spoke to the
army colonel in English. He permitted me to take Bua
home. She had become feeble with hunger and thirst.
When I returned to the graveyard after leaving Bua at
her home, there was suspicion in the eyes of the people:
a sort of hatred and a kind of strangeness. I went and sat
in a corner of the graveyard, a little unsure of myself.

Just before nightfall the military police pulled the curtain down on its own drama. People began to return to their houses. When I returned to Bua's house, I found the door locked and my suitcase and belongings kept at the door. I dragged my suitcase after me and came to the main road and sat down against the wall around the lake's shore. I had lost all hope when a stranger stopped and accosted me, 'Where do you want to go, memsaab?'

I tried to affect a smile.

'I want to stay in a houseboat for a night.'

'There are no guests any more in the houseboats, memsaab. There are no houseboats any more. But there's a man . . . he lives on one . . . it's his home.'

'Where?'

He pointed into the distance.

'There . . . that's Wazira's houseboat.'

'Whose?' I sprung up on my feet.

'Wazir Ali is his name. He's an old man.'

'Will you take me there? I will request him, plead with him; maybe he will let me stay . . . for just one night.'

A little taken aback by my request, he half-heartedly picked up my suitcase. 'Come then . . . but he does not accept guests . . . actually, nobody comes any more.' He kept talking as he walked. 'Forget the guests, memsaab, even the birds from Roos . . . and from where not . . . they used to come . . . now even they no longer come over to the lake.'

I did not know why but I was sure that this Wazir Ali must be the same man: the one who had stolen me when I was an infant, rather who I wished had stolen me. But as it turned out, this Wazir Ali was someone else. Even then he agreed to let me stay in his houseboat for the night. He even spread out a bed for me—on the floor. There weren't any engraved, chiselled walnut beds.

The next day I returned to the airport. Three times, at three different places, they opened all my luggage and rifled through my belongings. They poked through my bras and panties. A pain shot up through my chest, again. Everywhere there were two queues, two separate enclosures, for body searches. The way these women felt me up, it seemed they were lesbians, all of them. In the third enclosure they made me take off even my shoes and socks and felt me up all over again. And then they paused in their search and asked me, 'What's that?'

I had to say, 'A sanitary pad. I am chumming.'

It was then that I heard a voice rise from the adjoining enclosure. A little choked but familiar.

'Who's in there?' I asked, and nearly pushed my way into the enclosure. Right in front of me stood Bua. A ticket to Delhi flapped in her hand. The drawstrings of her salwar were untied and they had fallen around her ankles; she had pulled her shirt up and was screaming in a string-thin voice, 'This is the only place left to search . . . have a look . . . take a proper look!'

She clamped up when she saw me.

'What kind of a country have I come to? Is this really my country?'

And then she flopped down on her salwar gathered at her ankles, all life draining out of her.

Khalil's scream began to ring into my ears. 'What do you people want, enh? What do you want from us? Why don't you just let us be, leave us on our own? Now even our green has turned red . . . the grass growing on our earth has become red . . . enh . . .'

For Humra Quraishi

V

It never shows its face and never stops blubbering
A thought like a cricket, in the dreary silence of my soul
Keeps chirping—

Farewell

There was neither a name nor an address, just a simple note—scrawled in a running hand—in a simple envelope. Had Guru not picked up the doormat on opening the door, the envelope would have stayed unnoticed. He was afraid of the doormat being stolen. So he would pick the mat up from inside the door and drop it on the other side of the threshold when he came back to the room. Whoever had pushed the envelope under the door was not aware of this and the letter had slipped underneath the doormat.

Scrawled on the piece of paper were the words:

Yang Sui has come from Vietnam. Wants to meet up with you. We will be at Shyamal's place. Do come and bring your newly written poems.

Poems? Try as hard as he could, Gorakh Pandey could not fathom any meaning out of this. Poems? What poems? He wasn't a poet. Nor did he know of any poets in the hostel. Who was this letter for? He scanned it again, inspected the envelope: there were no giveaway greetings, no tell-tale salutations; no, not even a name on the envelope. He folded the letter and slipped it into the pocket of his trackpants. He groped under the bed for his sneakers, slipped them on and left for his run. That's what he did every morning—walked out of the hostel, cut through the college maidan, crossed the highway and ran two laps of the park on the other side and then back to the hostel. It was a matter of habit with him. And this kept Guru—a name his friends had fondly taken to calling him after the nickname of his namesake, the infamous Naxalite Gorakh Pandey—fit as a fiddle.

A couple of days later, the same thing happened again. Guru came back from his run and began to clean his room. He picked up the doormat to dust it and found another letter. It was just like the earlier one: a simple note in a simple envelope. This time too, the letter betrayed neither a name nor an address, not even a date. There was a salutation though, perhaps a lingering whiff of a relationship:

> *Dada, we missed you a lot. Yang Sui is off to Calcutta today and she is flying out from Calcutta itself. The other day she kept waiting for you. Her train will leave this evening. Come by 4.30, if you can. We will wait for you outside the station.*
>
> —*P*

The handwriting looked feminine at first sight. But then

he glanced over the initial again—the P was too bold, too firm to be either a Pushpa or a Preeti. Looked more like a P some man called Parthiv would sign off with. And it was then that he remembered the first letter he had forgotten in the pocket of his track pants. The track pants were now in the laundry. He pulled open the drawer of his writing table and dropped the letter into it.

For the next few moments the letter occupied his thoughts. He thought about it while sipping his tea, dwelt on it while devouring his breakfast. A small little explanation found an expression: somebody's having an affair . . . a romance maybe . . . with a girl from Vietnam . . . and he did not go to meet her . . . either the two lovers had had a spat or perhaps he was no longer interested in her and was simply bluffing. He kept nurturing the thought, embellishing it a little here, pruning it a little there, and by the time he reached the college for his classes, the small little explanation had sprung itself into a full-fledged story.

No more letters arrived after that. Every few days, whenever Guru would remember he would pick the doormat up and look underneath it. It became a sort of a habit. No, not exactly a habit—a curiosity perhaps. Or maybe the search for an answer—who was that letter for? But the answer always eluded him. And he finally gave up on it. There were far too many things happening in the city. The Naxalite movement was picking up speed. There would be some incident of violence every day—a bomb going off somewhere, an explosion ripping out the innards of the city someplace else. The attendance of students began to thin. Now, even the professors were absenting themselves from the classes. Most of Guru's time would now be spent either in the library or the canteen.

Something was afoot in the canteen, brewing in the hushed silence of his friends. Guru let it be. But when their conspiratorial silence began to cause him discomfort, he asked a friend. The friend took him outside the canteen into the college maidan, leaned into his ears and said, 'A meeting's scheduled to take place in the city. In Rajpur . . . perhaps . . .'

'What kind of a meeting?'

'Cultural . . . but who knows,' a surreptitious shrug of the shoulder, 'it may turn a different shade . . . maybe political.' He cast a furtive glance around and spoke again into Guru's ears, 'It is believed that Guru is coming for the meeting.'

'Who?'

'Your namesake, Gorakh Pandey!'

The other Gorakh Pandey was from Bihar as well, but during the Naxalite movement he had become really popular in Bengal. There was something about him, something about the way he wrote that could whip up a frenzy amongst the youth of his generation. The moment Gorakh Pandey wrote a new poem a current would ripple through the city, and boys and girls alike would regroup themselves and right under the nose of the vigilant police, would paste copies of his poems on every available surface. The youth would read his fiery poems in anti-establishment newspapers, off posters on trams and buses, and work themselves up into a hysteria.

And yet, nobody knew what Gorakh Pandey looked like. Nobody had seen him. The police would forever be on a lookout for him and would publish his photographs in newspapers at regular intervals, but never ever would two photographs be the same, and of the same man. Because the police was on a lookout, Gorakh would forever keep changing his guise. Some believed that none of the published photographs were his.

The Naxalbari movement was now spilling over the Bengal border into Bihar. Our Guru was an undergraduate student. He had nothing to do with any political movement, he had no affiliations whatsoever. No, not even by a far stretch. But being a student of literature he did peruse a few of his namesake's poems and if truth be told, he did find a suppressed anger pulsate through his spine.

Not so long ago, a friend of his had said while they were sitting in the canteen, 'Guru, you have to listen to him once . . . his words will put your soul on fire.'

'Have you?'

'God . . . if I was fortunate enough to have heard him do you think I would have been sitting here in front of you? His words would have set me afire, burnt me to cinders; my ashes would have been here in my place . . . on that plate . . .'

Guru left for the tryst with the infamous, incendiary Gorakh Pandey with that very friend. Nothing was ascertained though: Where would the meeting take place? How would it take place? Who all would be there? Nothing was certain. Not as yet.

They were only halfway to the venue when the traffic began to be diverted. And when they reached Badal Chowk it seemed as if the entire city had come to a standstill. Station Road was blockaded, off limits. A bomb had exploded at A.N. Chowk and the jeep of the police commissioner had been blown away. Fortunately the police commissioner had survived—a close shave. Guru and his friend got off the bus and walked back all the way to the hostel. It took them a few hours.

That night Guru was about to roll off to sleep when his eyes came to rest on the doormat. He shot out of bed and picked the mat off the floor. A letter! Yes there was a letter. Similar to the ones that he had found earlier: a simple note in a simple envelope. But this one was scrawled in a hurry:

You will find S behind St Agnes' Church. The car will be ready to take you straight to Kohima. There's not a moment to waste. Hurry!

–P

Guru kept looking at the letter, spinning off numerous threads to the story in his head. He entangled himself inextricably, and fell asleep, exhausted. In the wee hours of the morning, a hullaballoo woke him up. The police had cordoned the hostel off and everybody was being roused from their sleep and lined up outside. Every single room was being searched.

Suddenly a constable came running, 'Sir, we have found him, sir . . . he has swallowed cyanide.'

He looked to be twenty-six, certainly not more than twenty-seven. There was a well-trimmed beard on his face, it looked freshly groomed. Rimless glasses were still perched atop the bridge of his nose.

'In which room did you find him?' somebody asked.

'Room number fifty-one.'

That was the room next to Guru's.

'But who is he?' Guru asked.

'Don't you know him! The infamous Naxalite Gorakh Pandey!'

Guru stood rooted to the spot, stunned into silence.

'There were rumours that he was hiding somewhere in our city . . .'

'Gawd! Think of it . . . hiding in our very hostel and we had absolutely no idea!'

Guru's hand was in the pocket of his trackpants, his fingers clutching at the remnants of that first letter which had now been laundered clean along with his trousers.

While the investigating police officer tried to prepare a first listing of the evidence and findings at the scene of the crime, he showed the hostel warden a letter that he had found on the body of the deceased. A simple note without the simple envelope. Written in Bangla were the words:

Ek baar biday de Ma, ghoorey aashi!

Bid me farewell now, O Mother, I promise I will be back . . .**

*This is the first line of a popular Bengali patriotic song composed in the early twentieth century in honour of the boy-martyr, Khudiram Bose.

Swayamvar

When she opened her eyes, it was morning—pretty early in the morning.

She was a bit puzzled, a bit intrigued—how on earth had she fallen asleep in the first place? She had not taken the sleeping pills in spite of Swaran's insistence. She was absolutely relaxed, watching a movie on TV late into the night. She was really into the movies, the pulpy kind that had a lot of fights and thrills thrown in. She saw a few too many of them. And they all appeared real to her—the movies opened her world to the possibilities of all that could happen and yet, nothing really did. That's what life is about, she would often sigh. But the last night of her life she had wanted to spend fully awake. Then how did she fall asleep? How could sleep descend upon The Bomb? She was nothing but a 'mission', and how could a mission shut its eyes?

And then a thought found seed: maybe Swaran had

slipped a sleeping pill or two into her coffee. Swaran was her custodian. If she were to fail her mission or if her resolve weakened, Swaran was to shoot her down, then and there.

For a moment, anger pulsed through her veins. Her head buzzed in fury. How dare he? When she said no, she meant no—an absolute NO. She did not like anything being imposed on her. And trust was an absolute. She couldn't tolerate anybody doubting her, even for a moment. She knew her own constitution pretty well. She never ever made any impulsive decisions.

But the very next moment, her anger dissipated. She remembered last night—it was she herself who had made the coffee. She had in fact even asked Swaran if he wanted some. And Swaran had shaken his head in refusal.

He had been sitting at the table engrossed in divining solutions to algebraic equations. Quite a strange way to relax—but then, to each his own.

She remembered switching the TV off. And she remembered thinking about her mother when she had propped herself on the bed thereafter. It flicked on a switch inside and the scene of her mother being raped by the village headman in the coconut grove began to unspool before her eyes. The headman looked after the chief minister's interests in the village. She flicked the switch off. She had by now begun to pity her mother. And she hated this emotion called pity. The sickle the villagers used to chop the husk of coconuts was lying next to her. Why hadn't her mother simply picked it up and torn open the intestines of the man?

The scene wasn't complete. It was still floating in the salty water of her eyes. She got up and switched off the lights. She glanced at the watch strapped to her wrist. It appeared blurry but this much she could make out: the date was still the same. The day was yet to be over.

When she awoke, dawn had not yet broken but the sky had now begun to turn grey at its edges. But there was enough light to read the dial of her watch: a new number had scrolled up in the date window—a new day, a new date. She had so badly wanted to see the dates change, but she had slept the opportunity away. She kept lying in her bed. Had she really fallen asleep that early last night? She must have been stressed. There must have been a lot of agitation in her subconscious. Little wonder she had drifted away into sleep after she killed the lights. She resented being ruled by her subconscious. She heard the whoosh of the kerosene stove. Swaran must be up. Had he slept at all? He was an insomniac anyway, whether he slept or lay awake all night, he was always the same, like the notations in algebra. Come to think of it, his face looked like an algebraic equation, ears bent outwards at both ends. If you were to pull them together it would become the X and the nose—as if somebody had hung the Y upside down, an upside-down catapult. And the eyes . . . the eyes . . . she could not think of a suitable parallel in algebra. She smiled at the little ruse she had invented to amuse herself. Algebra used to give her the jitters when she was in school. Thank God she had quit school early. Her *taadi*-addict uncle had pulled her out.

The sound of rustling feet broke her thoughts. She looked up to find an entire equation of algebra standing at the door with a steaming cup of coffee. He looked as if he had stepped out of that photo that Najam Palli had framed on his wall: not a hair was out of place. Najam Palli was Swaran's friend. The first time she had seen him, he was lying in a bloody heap outside his own house. She had gone there looking for her *taadi*-addict uncle. And Najam Palli had been dumped outside his own door by the headman's cronies, beaten to a pulp. She had no idea Najam Palli was her uncle's younger brother, her younger uncle. She had never seen this uncle before. She had heard it said that during high tide he would row his dinghy through the bay into the village and the fishermen would stealthily go and meet him. She had also heard that Najam Palli's land had been bought by the chief minister. The village headman was the chief minister's man. The chief minister was the prime minister's man. She had heard that the prime minister, who lived in far-flung Delhi, was afraid of this Najam Palli of Sukha Puram, this country of parched earth, this place of droughts.

She went for a bath after finishing her coffee. She kept sitting under the shower for quite a while. Nothing of much significance crossed her mind. Just plain, simple, ordinary things: like the shape of the bar of soap she was using. She did not take to it. She thought of changing it the next time she showered. Next time? There wasn't going to be a next time. This was her last shower, her last bath, her last toilette. The shower dried up in the middle of her bath. An irritation crept in; bloody shit . . . tomorrow . . . tomorrow she would go and sort this thing out with the landlord. Tomorrow? Once again tomorrow? The shot of the film had to be cut in the middle. And slowly a feeling began to unspool, the feeling of the last day, her last day. And as the feeling began to slowly sink into her, she could detect an unfolding sense of drama—faint at the moment, the full impact of which she was yet to discover. The shower sputtered, coughed and then began to disgorge water all over again. Part of the soap lather that had dried on her skin had now begun to come off her body, like the discarded skin of a moulting snake.

Thoughts are like traffic on a busy street. A thought comes honking from behind and overtakes another. She had not brought a towel. She had stepped into the bathroom without one. She had never forgotten it before. Was she stressed? Subconsciously? Once again she felt irritated by her subconscious. She was not willing to believe that there was any kind of stress within her. In the sudden absence of the sound of gushing water another thought ushered itself in. She felt like doing something that she had never ever done before. Something that would satiate her desires, fulfil her dreams, something that would make her life worth having lived. Something that would be a befitting climax, a beautiful 'The End' to the film of her life. A fleeting desire took root—to get her photograph clicked. And by the time she stepped out of the bathroom, the desire had bloomed. She was all set, decided. She went to tell Swaran but he had gone for his bath.

On the way to the photographer they passed the Shiva temple. Swaran looked in her direction. Should he ask the driver to stop the taxi or should he not? He knew that she came to this temple, not often, just once in a while. She too looked in his direction and with the slight shake of her head told him not to. She thought the idea meaningless, or perhaps God alone knew why she did not feel up to it. Perhaps she was scared—she knew she could not gather the courage to face her God. Or perhaps the thought of grovelling before her God to grant her the courage to execute her mission made her an object of pity. Pity, that same creepy feeling.

By the time they reached the photographer's studio, she had made one more decision—to write Raj Kumari a letter. Raj Kumari, her friend from the village. The last time she saw her was over a year ago, grinding her life away in marital unhappiness, eking out a stifling, miserable existence. She had slapped her when she saw the tears in her eyes. Bloody bitch! She had cursed at her a little more. Raj Kumari's jaws had dropped, 'O Ma! Look at you cussing! Such a foul tongue . . . you are cussing the way my husband does!'

'He cusses at you?

'Yes . . . the headman cusses at him . . . he cusses at me!'

She rolled down the window and spat outside. The taste on her tongue was turning bitter; she had no idea why. She guzzled down two tall glasses of water the moment she reached the studio of Babulal photographer. Babulal's son was a recent convert to the ways of the city; he had just returned from one. He was looking dashing in a body-hugging jersey. He sprinkled a lot of English words in his conversation. She liked him. He had brought a newfangled camera with him. It was he who made her sit on the stool. It was he who made her pose for the camera. He took a long time doing so, and told her his mile-long-tongue-twister of a name only to quip in English, 'You can just call me AK; that's what people call me!'

She realized that today Swaran was smoking more than he normally did. This was the second consecutive cigarette that he had pulled out of his pocket. Suddenly he spoke, 'AK, there's a political gathering in Sukhampur this evening. The PM is coming with the CM. Want to come along?'

'Will I be allowed in?' AK asked.

'I will be the reporter with the copy-pencil in my hand, all you need to do is hang the camera around your neck. I will tell them that you are with me.'

'You got a pass?'

'I'm your pass!' She laughed for the first time in twenty-four hours. She liked the informality with which she could treat him.

That evening at the political gathering, the turnout was massive—a sea of people. Her heart began to pound in her chest. She could hear it pounding loudly, distinctly, as if she were listening to a walkman. Her jaws began to ache. If there was something in her subconscious . . . she held on to it with her teeth, trying to crush it between her molars with all her might. Whenever Swaran looked at her, he found her jaws moving. Something was being ground. Was it her anger? Her fear, perhaps? Or was it her scream that she held on to, not letting it escape her mouth?

A sudden uproar: the PM had arrived. The huge floodlights sprung to life. A cavalcade, about eight or ten cars long, screeched to a halt. Plumes of dust could be seen eddying up in the backlight. The cars could not be seen but a horde of heads could be seen rolling towards the main gate. The volume of the walkman inside her head began to turn up. AK was in the lead.

Swaran took the garland out of the bag slung across his shoulder and thrust it toward her. But she did not see it. Her hands and feet were turning to stone. Her blood circulation was beginning to grind to a halt. Swaran was concerned. He was her keeper, her steward. He had to steer her back on the right path, keep her on the right track. He shuffled closer to her. She was juggling numerous problems of algebra in her mind. Now things began to gather pace.

She could suddenly make out the face of the PM at the surge of the crowd that had slowly begun to ebb behind him. And she speared his face with her gaze as a fish is speared in a hook.

Her jaws stopped grinding. The bone of fear was crunched, finally. And slowly the circulation of blood began to return to normal. Swaran looked at her again. Her face was now relaxed. There was no sign of fear on it, no sign of conflict either. But the way she had locked her gaze on to the face of the PM, he found it a bit strange.

As if she had suddenly fallen in love with him. Her eyes had begun to smile as if they were caressing him. And she began to move towards the PM with a sense of fulfilment. The headman was trying to control the crowd, along with the volunteers. And she was floating towards the PM.

A number of eyes lit up on his face, on his ears, on his forehead, on his chin, his bottom. She could see everything, see the universe at play. She took the garland from Swaran and put it around his neck as if it was her own swayamvar and she had finally chosen her soulmate—together in life and together in death.

An explosion burst open the seams of time and they both transgressed time together to enter the annals of history—immortalized for all time to come.

Half a Rupee

When Chandu ran away from Class Three, he paused for breath only after he had reached Bombay. It is an altogether different story that he now works at the minister's bungalow. But he still remembers every little thing.

For three straight days and three straight nights he had been awake. When he finally did fall asleep on a footpath in Byculla, the havildar kicked him awake right in the middle of the night to ask, 'So bhai, which UP have you come from?'

'Faizabad.'

'Accha . . . one *atthanni* gimme . . . no free sleeping on this footpath . . . what?'

For a moment Chandu thought that he had seen the man in some phillum. They talked like that only in the phillum.

'I don't have any money . . . if I did, I wouldn't have come to the city.'

149

'This no city. This is Mumbai—what? This is metropolis. Come, one *atthanni* gimme.'

Jhumru who was sleeping next to him woke up, 'Aye Deva . . . why you troubling the boy? Here, take this *atthanni* and let us sleep.'

Jhumru picked up a half-rupee coin from the handful of change under his pillow and flung it in the havildar's direction. Deva caught it in mid-air and said, 'Saala miser, paying for him—he is your own or what?' He moved ahead clinking the *atthannis* in the palm of his hand.

Chandu failed to understand what kind of a city this was—it kicked you but it also caressed you. Sleep did not come to him the rest of that night.

He bumped into Jhumru again the next morning.

'So . . . coming straight from the village? With so much oil in your hair you thinking of becoming a hero?'

'No, yaar . . . I've—'

Jhumru flew off the handle, 'Whores have yaars. Call me chacha; everybody here calls me chacha—Jhumru chacha.'

Chandu swallowed his own spit and thought it wise to keep his quiet.

Jhumru said, 'Deva will be here again. For allowing you to sleep here he takes money . . . one week one *atthanni*.'

Blood drained from Chandu's face, revealing a yellow, jaundiced face.

'You want to live here in this city—don't become a turmeric. Become chilli, red hot chilli.'

After a pause, Jhumru said again, 'Coming to Chowpatti? Big leader, big speech . . . five rupees we will get.'

'Five rupees? What do we need to do to earn that?'

'Listen to leader's speech. Clapping-clapping. And shouting "Jai ho!" Nothing more.'

Chandu smiled, 'Five rupees for this?'

'Yes! But fifty per cent mine. Listen, palty giving ten rupees to Deva. He cutting five rupees and only giving five rupees to me. He getting order of fifty people from our footpath. I arranging all. Understand?'

Chandu nodded his head. 'Ho.' That was the first Marathi word that he had learnt.

Chandu felt it all over again: what kind of a city was this—it fed you and also bit you.

Jhumru said, 'We all like komri only.'

'Komri, what is komri?'

'Komri meaning chicken. This city throwing foodgrain. And we pecking tuk-tuk like chicken. And when we becoming fat and big on free food then we getting chopped.'

'Who chops us?'

'The king-log.'

'And who are they?'

'In this city, king only two kind of people. Firstly—the palty people. Giving talk. Giving speech. Giving note. Taking vote. And secondly—the gun-and-knife people. Taking money. Not taking lives. But sometimes, taking lives, giving money.'

'You mean the goonda-log?'

'Goonda-log, they both. Only difference—ishtyle.'

It did not take Chandu long to learn the ways of the metropolis.

A man from the party had come with Deva the next time. He counted the men and asked, 'When Netaji says, "Mumbai konachi"—who does Mumbai belong to—what are you all going to say?'

Everybody shouted in unison, 'Mumbai aamchi!'

'Aye Madrasi . . . say it in Marathi, okay, not in Tamil. What are you going to say?'

'Mumbai aamchi!'

'Good!'

When he went away Chandu said to Deva, 'Bhau!' He had heard people call Deva 'bhau', big brother. Deva's features softened. 'Bhau how much does this party-wallah get for one man?'

Deva's face hardened again, 'What is it to you? You getting your five *atthannis* or no?'

'Five *atthannis* are hardly anything, Bhau.'

'Enough for five week sleeping rent or no?'

'For sleeping, yes, but what does one eat, Bhau?'

'I calling you here or what? Which UP you coming from—tell, tell.'

'Faizabad.'

'Who giving you food in Faizabad? Who? Tell, tell.'

Chandu uttered such a big lie that he himself shuddered under its impact. He began to stutter, 'We—we were farmhands, a . . . a family of poor workers on daily wages, Bhau. And suddenly terrorists surrounded us and taar-taar-taar-taar they . . . they shot my full family down . . . brother, sister, mother, father . . . everybody.'

He could not think of anything further. He had begun to quiver. But Bhau's face had softened. He thought that Chandu was telling the truth.

'I seeing what I can doing. Finding you some work later. You knowing some reading-writing or what?'

'I can . . . I was in Class Three when I ran away from the village school.'

'Can write your name?'

'Ho!'

'And also mine—can?'

'Ho!'

'Fine, then! From tomorrow you working with me. I having to fill my dairy for whole week. My Hindi not so good. National language, no? Government allowing writing only in that. I tell I know, when getting job. But that saala, there is one man who taking four *atthanni* for filling the dairy only one time one week. In this metropolis nobody doing anything for nothing. What?'

Chandu's work was done. But still he asked, 'Bhau, why do you always do all your counting in *atthannis*?'

Bhau laughed halfway through and said, 'Because "common man" like us only having half of things—half-plate eating, half-night sleeping, half laughing, half crying, half living and also half dying. This *atthanni* never becomes full rupiah.' He paused a while and then said, 'This top type thinking or what?' And then added in a hushed tone, 'A Naxalite told me this.'

Chandu started following Bhau around like a reporter. Whatever he did, he would ask Chandu to write it down. Chandu started living with Bhau in his kholi. At times, he would even cook a meal and take it to wherever Bhau was on duty.

A little below Byculla, next to Sarvi Hotel, is a small, narrow lane. A man hawked his wares on a *khomcha* right at the head of the lane. He looked very Urdu-speaking. He did not have a license. Bhau found out one day, took his diary out and asked him, 'What you selling?'

The man spoke in a pronounced Lucknavi style, '*Khamire ki gulqandiyan.*'

Bhau was startled, 'What?'

'Fermented *gulqand*, sahib.'

'But what is that?'

'Rose-petal . . . try it for yourself.'

'Hoon!' he savoured the offering. '*Apan chaa naav kay?*' he asked in Marathi. 'What's your name?'

'Ishaqul Rahman Siddiqi.'

Bhau raised his voice a little, 'Say it in Hindi . . . understand . . . say your name in Hindi.'

The man said it all over again, 'Ishaqul Rahman Siddiqi.'

Bhau drew in a deep breath, poised his pencil over his diary and asked him, 'Short e or long ee?'

'What's that, sahib?' Between his Urdu and Bhau's Hindi, things were lost.

Bhau slapped his diary shut and said, 'Look . . . I am

letting you go this time, but this is not going in my report. In my report your name entering Babu and you selling aloo. What?'

By then Chandu had arrived. Bhau handed over his diary and pencil and said, 'Write it down! Name—Babu. Business—selling aloo. Chandu, take four *atthanni* from him.' Saying this, he moved on.

Something similar happened another time as well. Chandu was in the grip of fever that day, so he was unable to accompany Bhau. Bhau came back and told him the story.

'You knowing that Vinayak Rao Road.'

This was when Deva had been transferred to Warden Road; he now lived in a kholi in Worli.

Chandu egged him on, 'So, what happened at Vinayak Rao Road?' He was now familiar with the roads of the metropolis.

'Cow dying.'

'Whom did it belong to?'

'Having no idea. One of those cow-log that keeping wandering on the roads with their families. Bloody that cow coming and dying on that road. Such difficult name—Vinayak Rao Patwardhan Road. Who writing it all down? And that too in Hindi?'

Chandu burst out laughing.

'Then what did you do?'

'Taking two hours. But I dragging the cow by catching the tail. Dragging and dragging. My breath becoming difficult and difficult but finally I succeeding in bringing the dead cow onto next road. Taking me two hours.'

'But why did you drag it to the next road?'

'Next road name is Bapu Road. Easy writing.'

'Who gave you the *atthanni*?'

'The man in front of whose house the cow dying.'

Bhau and Chandu's friendship was now quite a few years old. And in those few years, Bhau had made him accept and quit numerous jobs. Then he called in a favour with a party-wallah and got him appointed as a watchman at the residence of a minister.

Chandu had by now become a proper Mumbaiite. The minister had a lot of trust in him, enough to send him on a number of personal errands. It had now become Chandu's job to fetch the minister's briefcase. Chandu had now left counting in *atthannis* behind. But at times some give and take of *atthannis* still did take place.

Then one day there was a huge explosion at the bungalow.

The minister was in his office. Startled, he nearly shot up from his chair. And the very next moment, Chandu fell at his feet. Right behind him was a man wielding an AK-47.

'What? What's the meaning of this?' He turned to look at Chandu and admonished him, 'Why—why did you let this man walk in, Chandu?'

'I—I did not, sahib, the man just pushed me in.' Chandu wobbled and staggered to his feet at gunpoint.

'Who are you, brother?' the minister had by now registered the gun in the hands of the intruder and his voice had softened a notch.

'Who do you think I am?'

'A terrorist . . . I think.'

The terrorist smiled. The minister did too.

'Why are you holding him?' The minister gestured towards Chandu.

'He is my hostage.'

'Mine too,' the minister quipped.

'Really? Your hostage? How can he be a hostage when he was roaming freely outside?'

'Unlike you, I don't have to wield a gun to take a hostage.'

'Then how do you keep a hold on them?'

'First with notes, then with votes. I hold them captive for five years.'

'And after that?'

'A renewal. Every five years we renew our term for another five years.'

The terrorist changed his stance, took hold of his gun and said, 'This leave-and-license system is not going to work any more.'

'Then what will?'

'Why don't you ask him? Between you and me, only he is common. The common man!'

The minister asked Chandu, 'Tell me, what do you prefer—death by bullet, die once and for all . . . or—'

The terrorist stepped forward, 'Or die a little every day . . . bit by bit . . . die every five years?'

Chandu paused a little, stole a look at the two of them

and then thrust his hand in his pocket.

The terrorist threatened, 'What's in your pocket?'

Chandu was not flustered; he said, 'Nothing . . . just an *atthanni* . . . I want to toss and find the answer.'

He took a step forward. And the moment he tossed the coin up in the air they both yelled, almost in unison, 'Heads.'

Thankfully the *atthanni* did not come back down. Or else . . . on both its sides it would have been Chandu's head.

VI

Growing up, I was struck by a thought
Shouldn't I ask around how important is it
To grow up—

Gagi and Superman

Superman comics and videocassettes had begun to pile up in my house. In the beginning these piles were to be seen only in the children's room. But slowly they began to slide out of their rooms and encroach on my bookshelves too. If I pulled out a book, 2–3 Superman comics would topple down. For a few moments I would wonder what to do with them and then I would deliberately shove them behind my books. A few times I even told Umi, 'Why don't you sell them off to the kabadi-wallah?'

'Mummy . . . no!' Buchki, my little one, just sprang up from nowhere. Even now she had a Superman book in her hand. She looked at me and said in English, 'Papa! How can you! Superman is Superman! Why don't you sell a few of your own books? Now, even Superman needs a little space.'

Umi sauntered away laughing, 'The videocassettes are yet to come. Her room is already overflowing.'

'But where did all these come from?'

'Gagi! She's the one, the supplier.'

Gagi was the same age as my daughter and in the same grade too, but she went to a different school. About half her growing-up years had been spent in our house, and the rest in her own parents'—Vikas Desai's and Aruna Raje's.

She lived for only eleven years.

All day long all these kids ever did was watch Superman on TV and read Superman comics. If I said something they would straightaway put their marksheets in front of me—now you cannot reprimand children who got straight As in every subject. And these kids excelled not only in studies but in everything they did.

One day I really got fed up and scolded all of them roundly. Gagi was quick to retort, 'Uncle, Superman is like God. He can do anything, just like God.' Gagi was quick of wit.

She was only nine years old when she was diagnosed with cancer—bone cancer. Poor Puggi and Buchki. Puggi was Basu Bhattacharya's daughter. Because all three of us—Vikas, Basu and I—were filmmakers, it was but natural for the kids to get together often at one of our places. And because my wife did not stay with me, they felt a little more free in my house, a little more independent. So my house had become their playground.

Once we all happened to be in Bangalore together. Vikas was very fond of swimming. He would spend most of his free time in the swimming pool. He would teach the kids to swim too and generally horse around with them in the pool. He was a little on the heavier side. Gagi once said, 'Papa, you are so fat . . . how come you don't sink in the pool?'

'Water is very strong, sweetie. It can carry huge ships.'

'But how come my wristwatch sank then?'

Vikas was without an answer. He stole a look at Aruna and she burst out laughing. Vikas was visibly embarrassed, so we left the poolside and retired to our room. When a little later Vikas returned with Gagi, she was limping a little. The limp did not augur well. It was the first hint of the impending tragedy.

When Gagi found it increasingly difficult to walk, treatment for her leg started. A number of different kinds of shoes were made and tried on her. But the pain in her legs refused to subside. She was very fond of learning Kathak. That was the first thing that had to stop. But she would still vocalize the rhythm. She would dance with her mouth while stumbling towards the car, while scrambling down the stairs: 'Tar kut taa thaee . . . tar . . . kut taa thaee . . . thaee . . .'

Music was in her blood, in her genes. Her father's uncle, Vasant Desai, was a famous music composer. When the pain in her legs became nagging and a constant occurrence, Gagi became irregular at school. But Kathak was one thing that she really missed and she expressed her desire to resume her dancing lessons. Aruna arranged for a dance master to give her private lessons at home. But though Gagi put on her dancing bells, her ghungroos, she could never really dance again—she could only walk in them.

For the first time now, Dr Adhikari became suspicious— he began to suspect that the problem was not in her legs or her knees but in the marrow of her shin bones. When X-rays were inconclusive, other tests began to be performed. Vasant shifted into his uncle Vasant Desai's house which was just opposite Jaslok Hospital, right on Peddar Road.

Dr Adhikari had reached a diagnosis but he kept hoping against hope, conducting test after test; but one day finally he had to place the medical reports in front of Vikas and Aruna. Gagi was sitting outside the doctor's chambers. Vikas and Aruna sat inside in stunned silence. Gagi's cancer was now confirmed without any doubt. Before Vikas and Aruna left the doctor's chambers they swore that they would never shed a tear in front of Gagi. The two of them fought the calamity with great fortitude. We did not see either of them shed a single tear in Gagi's lifetime—whatever was left of it—however often and however much they might have cried in the privacy of their own room.

Old friends and new playmates, uncles and aunties, games and videos, dancing monkeys and waltzing bears and what not were paraded through Gagi's room. Gagi was not given a moment to think, to mull over her disease. Vikas and Aruna did not let the grimness of the hospital waft into their house. I would often marvel at their spirit. Gagi had become an expert in *antakshari*. When medicines stopped working the doctors began to talk about operating on Gagi's leg. Vikas and Aruna took her to America. Now Gagi knew that she had cancer.

'But why in my leg Papa?'

'It's the cancer of the bones, beta. It's in the bone of the leg. They are going to operate on your bone, scrape it out of your bone before it spreads.'

In America, Gagi's treatment stretched over a few months. She lost all her hair to chemotherapy. She would dread running her hand over her hairless pate and look at her parents through eyes filled with fear. Aruna and Vikas would do their best to laugh it all off.

'Baldy . . . don't you be scared . . . your hair's gonna grow back in a matter of months.'

'I love you this way. This is the current trend. The in-thing. Haven't you heard?'

'Hi, Yul Brynner!'

I think Gagi had immense faith in her parents' laughter and believed that she was going to get better soon. That was the hope the doctors in America had rekindled in her when they plastered up the leg they had operated upon and sent her back to India.

But soon after her return from America, a foul, putrid smell began to emanate from her leg. She was in great pain. This time instead of Dr Adhikari another doctor was consulted. He had the plaster on her leg cut open. Her leg was festering with pus. The doctors were of the opinion that it was not cancer, it could not be cancer, but nobody was able to treat her back to health. Doctors began to be changed like medicines on their prescriptions. Within three months they sawed her leg off in the fear that the cancer might raise its ugly head again. The amputated limb was cremated in an electric crematorium with all the rites accorded to the dead.

When Gagi's glance climbed off the ceiling, she asked in a very quiet voice, 'Papa, why is God punishing me? I haven't ever done anything bad.'

Aruna had placed an icon of Krishna in her room. She would light joss sticks and the flame in the lamp would be kept up all through the day and the night in front of it. They had given up eating meat or fish as penance. However, when Gagi asked for kebabs or tikkas they would never refuse her. They had even asked her doctor and taken his permission.

One day when a new doctor entered her room, Gagi asked, 'You have changed the doctor again, Papa?'

'Yes, beta . . . that doctor could not do anything.'

She looked at the Krishna idol in the room and said, 'This god too can't do anything . . . isn't there another god, Papa?'

It wasn't like Aruna to say this, but somehow she just blurted out, 'He's like Superman only, beta . . . in the books he can do everything.'

Ghugu and Jamuni

High up on the branches of the tall, leafy suru tree, Ghugu would stealthily perch himself and patiently lie in wait for a glimpse of his beloved, every day. She would fly in from the orchard side, strutting her colorful plumes, carelessly trolling his patch of the sky. He had fallen in love with the kite, fallen in love with its shimmer of yellow and purple. He would sit mesmerized, watching her soar and dive, now to this rhythm, now to that. He really thought her to be a bird.

A number of times, he would flap his wings and fly past her, tweeting sweet nothings into her ears: 'The colours on your two wings are not the same . . . one's a brilliant yellow and the other is just the shade of ripe jamun berries I so love! May I call you Jamuni? You are so pretty!' And every time she would flutter her wings and fly away in one smooth move. He thought it to be her bashfulness. Once he had even invited her to his nest.

But she flounced away from him, soared away into the vast expanse of the sky—in silence, absolute silence. No chirp, no cheep, not even a tiny little tweet. Whenever he winged himself near her, she would prance away. Now he had learned to keep his distance, and whooped at her from a respectable distance: 'You look lovely when you strut about like this!' But even then she did not utter a single coo. And he yearned and longed to hear her voice—a trill, a tweet or a chirp—anything at all.

Her thoughts haunted him throughout the day and he kept hovering over the orchard. That was the direction she always flew in from. His eyes would scan the rooftops, the trees, the entire horizon—maybe he would get a glimpse of her, spot her roosting on the branch of some tree, or perhaps find her pecking on some rooftop. He would even forget to feed. He flew for hours on end with a grain or two stashed in his beak—thinking he would feed them to her when he found her. He had begun to hoard tufts of grass, lengths of thread. He was thinking of building a nest, to bring her home. The male of the species always did so. He wanted his to be the best, better than anyone else's.

And then, a few days later, he got to know that she wasn't a free bird. She was someone else's prisoner, tied at the back with a bright glistening string—thin as a thread, and pretty sharp. His wing had brushed against it, only once—and the thread had cut right through it. A few feathers had cut clean from his wing, and begun to sashay down to earth. It was then that it hit him—the realization—that she wasn't a free bird. She came with strings attached, a string that someone else pulled. That must be the reason she did not respond to his gestures, that must be the reason she did not make a single sound. Perhaps she was scared of her owner.

Her owner would let her fly for a while in the open but when a bird tried to come close to her, he would pull on her string and haul her back to his roof, take her by her ears and banish her into her cage. He had seen him holding her ears but where on earth did he keep her cage? If only he knew . . . if only he could find out . . . he could then at least try to free her.

That day too he sat high up in the branches of the tall suru tree. It was then that he saw the clouds, gathering ominously, rising together in a silent pact. He knew the clouds always belched out the wind in their bellies before they rained down. The wind would soon pick up speed, and no bird would dare fly with such a wind under its wings—not even someone as strong of feather as the crow. His Jamuni surely would not be able to withstand such a wind, such gusts. Her constitution was too delicate. And she had just spread her wings and flown off her roof. She was still finding her winghold, still seeking her balance in the sky. The winds were becoming increasingly strong, rattling the doors and windows. Ghugu flew to warn the kite—all care for his own safety tossed to the winds; his only concern was for his Jamuni. And then a strong gust of wind slapped his wings, tossed him around. He was still far away from his Jamuni but he kept flapping his wings, kept propelling himself forward, steering himself in the direction, kept squawking at her, 'Go back Jamuni . . . head back home . . . Jamuni! A storm's brewing . . . the clouds are soon going to burst . . . and the rain, you would—' Something lodged itself in his throat—the wind began to push him backwards. He could hardly see in the gathering darkness but he could still steer himself in the general direction of her house. The clouds now began to swoop down on him and the gust became too strong. He suddenly lost his balance. All his flapping was of no use. He was falling freely, rapidly losing his altitude—and then the wind picked him up once again and dashed him against an electric pole. That was when he lost consciousness.

When he returned to his senses, he found himself inside a wooden almirah, enveloped in soft clothes. It was still raining. He could make that much out from the dampness in the air. The pitter-patter of the raindrops was distant but distinct. And a strange smell arose from his body—the kind that he found when he alighted on the skylight of that hospital across the road. He could also hear the voices of children. And then it all came back to him. He remembered colliding against the electric pole. Some kind child must have found him. It must have been the kid who was looking after him. He closed his eyes as the pain shot up his little body. This pain he could bear, but what about the other pain, the one that refused to be healed? The moment he closed his eyes, Jamuni's face sprung to his mind. Was she alive? God forbid she had fallen in the storm. Did she manage to reach her home safely? He kept his eyes shut, kept nursing his pain—and the pain kept him alive.

After a few days in the almirah he was transferred to a wiry cage which was hung up in the balcony. He liked the feel of the sun on his feathers. He felt alive, felt life returning to his wings. He still couldn't flap his wings as he could earlier but he was now able to spread them. The pain had not all gone away, not yet, a little still remained in his shoulders.

Within a couple of days, he identified the voices of the other birds, and felt good. He was still in the same old neighbourhood, still on the very same side of the orchard from where Jamuni would fly in. A new hope began to throb in his veins, renewing his zest for life.

Days passed in waiting. He had begun to tweet and prattle all to himself, intermittently calling out to Jamuni: 'For a few days I will be here, staying with a few children . . . down here in the building, in Montu's house . . . don't look for me in the sky!'

'How have you been, Jamuni?'

'Where are you, Jamuni? Jamuni!'

And then, one day, finally he did spot the familiar half yellow half purple figure, high up there in the sky. And what a knot he wound himself in! He frantically began to flap about in his cage, squealing, pleading, clamouring to be let out. But there was nobody in the house to hear his pleas. He kept banging against the bars of his prison. His cage kept swinging, but that was all. He squawked, he cawed, he whistled and hooted—but Jamuni did not even cast a glance downwards in his direction.

A few minutes later, Jamuni disappeared from his sight. And then when he spotted her again she was frenziedly gliding down towards the bazaar. Her string was hanging down limply behind her. She must have broken free from her captivity. For him—to be with him! Slowly but surely, she had begun her descent. And below on the ground, a few kids had begun to run, jumping up now and then to try and catch her trailing string. Ghugu called out to her but his voice did not reach her. It got drowned in the cacophony of the bazaar and the shouts of the children. Then suddenly a big kid grabbed her string and ran into the narrow lane. He saw Jamuni straining to break away from him, trying to soar up, to fly away. But the kid's grasp on the string was very strong. She just couldn't break free, not this time.

And then . . .

Ghugu would not have been able to dream up what happened next, not ever. His heart skipped a beat. Montu ran into the house, brandishing Jamuni, his Jamuni.

'Ma . . . Ma . . . look, look! A patang . . . I found a patang!'

It was then that he got to know—his Jamuni already had a name: Patang. Everybody looked at her affectionately. Montu put her up on the wall in the balcony—the same balcony where Ghugu's cage was hung. All through the night, he kept calling out to her: 'Jamuni . . . Patang . . . Jamuni!' But she did not make a single sound, just swayed with the wind a couple of times. That was all.

Ghugu understood. She must have been born mute. That was why she never chirped, never cheeped, never tweeted, never said anything to him.

The Orange

Mamu, Amjad's maternal uncle, had a wonderful style of telling a story. He would start telling a story while talking about something else, and start talking about something else while telling a story. And quite effortlessly too.

'So, when in the beginning spacecrafts from the outer worlds came to study our solar system,' he said, 'they found this round earth of ours like an orange, but a blue and green orange . . .'

Amjad's attention once again went to his orange.

About two or three days ago, some oranges had been brought into the house. One orange fell to everybody's lot, but for Amjad's. He had a cough and cold and was also running a little fever. Amjad began to throw a tantrum and Ammi yielded. She let him have one, but he was forbidden to eat it.

'Don't eat it now. Till your cold gets better and your fever subsides just let it lie here.'

Amjad was consoled: at least he had not been deprived of his share. But now the orange had begun to lose its sheen—it did not look as fresh and lustrous as it had two days ago.

Mamu was still talking about the orange.

'The colour blue fascinated these men from the outer worlds and they deduced from its blue colour that more than two-thirds of this earth was made up of seas of water. And then they also found similar strips of blue running across the dry surface of the earth—as if the water from the seas were flowing into them . . . into those rivers . . .'

'But, Mamu, it's just the opposite . . . the waters from the rivers flow into the sea, not the other way round.'

'Oh . . . one thing you have forgotten . . . they were looking at the earth from way, way up. Now when you are looking at things from that far up, can you make out which way the flow is? You can't blame them, can you? All they saw were the colours . . . as if the earth was sprayed by colours . . . like this—'

Mamu pulled up the sleeve of his shirt to reveal a spidery spread of blue veins on his fat arms. Amjad did not find such a spidery web on his orange but yes, the fresh lustrous rind of the fruit had begun to feel soft to his touch and he could see grey–black spots threatening to burst out on the surface, like the ones on the face of his other uncle, his old, weathered Phupa.

Mamu's stories would run at a feverish pace for days on end. He would never give up on pushing the frontiers of his stories further, stretching them out over a few days.

He would move the end a notch further and yet further. But this time he moved up not a few days, but jumped ahead a few centuries.

'As the spacecrafts kept returning to their observation posts above the earth at regular intervals of centuries, the condition of the orange kept deteriorating, kept worsening. It went from bad to worse, from worse to worst. They flew closer to the earth . . . and found beautiful jungles. At places they found boxes of settlements, and inside those boxes they found earthlings, crawling like small little insects. But those boxes were few and far between, far away from each other.'

That day, Amjad picked up his orange and hid it behind the flower vase. He was not willing to let anybody throw it away till he got a fresh one in its place. Amjad's fever too was stretching out, like Mamu's stories, over days. The next instalment of Mamu's story began the next day.

'So I was telling you . . . yes, after another hundred years, another spacecraft came and swooped closer to the orange. This time it took them some time to find the blue orange. There was a lot of dust in the atmosphere. A thin thread of ozone had begun to leak out and float like a piece of cloud. On closer inspection they found that because of the constant travel of the earthlings, permanent lines were scrawled all over the planet. These lines started off at one settlement and disappeared into another. And on these scrawls, the earthlings had begun to move faster. It seemed as if one earthling had hauled another earthling on his back and had begun to run. Perhaps the earthlings had learnt to ride animals.

The settlements too had expanded and multiplied. At places they could see small golden suns burning: the earthlings had discovered fire. But where they had seen jungles once, now they found rivers of smoke, spiralling skywards. Perhaps the earthlings were burning jungles to clear more land for themselves, to build more of their boxes. The orange of the earth was no longer looking as fresh and lustrous and as inviting as those travellers before them had remarked.'

Amjad knew the secret. He had discovered the pricks in his orange, tiny holes, and had seen long queues of little ants crawling in and out of those holes. Where he had earlier seen spots of discolour now he found black and white mouldy overgrowth.

Mamu had once again flown away in his spacecraft. A few days later when he returned with his story a few more centuries had gone by.

'When those people of the spacecraft returned this time, they found the earth—which only a few centuries earlier they had discovered to be a lustrous planet, full of freshness—was wrapped in a thin film of poisonous gases. The layer of ozone was threadbare, like the cloth off the back of a poor beggar. And the atmosphere below it was filled with smoke and radioactive noise pollution. Only a few patches of green forest remained. The boxes of civilization had multiplied many times over and now covered the entire land. The entire earth was crawling with insects.'

Amjad's orange was now completely rotten and infested with worms and insects that kept biting into it and devouring it.

VII

I run and I run to keep in step
But look at this life
How quickly it marches on—

Under the Earth

He had no idea how long he had been lying in the darkness. When he slowly came back into consciousness he felt the ground beneath him quivering. After what seemed to him like a long time, the ground stopped shaking. It was only then that he opened his eyes for the first time. He was enveloped in darkness.

The ground had begun to shake again. He willed it to stop and then opened his eyes for the second time. He tried to stand up but the huge concrete slab on his back once again pinned him to the ground. He could not see anything in the dark.

When he opened his eyes again, he found both his hands burrowed into the earth. This time he let his head lie on the ground. Slowly his consciousness tossed and turned on its side and he remembered the earthquake— and he felt the ground quake all over again.

He was fast asleep when his bedstead had begun to shake. The continuous thud-thud kept drumming into his ears. The steel almirah had begun to quiver in the corner of the room as if in the grip of a malarial fever. He could hear the clanging of the utensils in the kitchen, faint at first and then clanking on the floor, rolling, crashing against the wall. At first he was a little scared at the strange sounds and then suddenly it all sank in—it was an earthquake. He had shot up from his bed, tried to switch the light on. It flickered to life, deigned to glow for a moment dully, and then died out. He could now hear the panicky cries of his neighbours. He had pushed the door open and ran out. The lift was not working. Somebody had switched the mains off. He ran for the stairs. There was absolute bedlam. Women were screaming. More and more people were pouring into the stairwell, running out of their homes, bounding down the stairs towards safety. He did not even realize how quickly he had climbed down the first two floors. On the landing of the next floor he felt bits and pieces of plaster, ripped off the ceiling above, fall on his head. The staircase had begun to tremble. The earthquake was perhaps rumbling through the ground right now, or maybe it was burping. Or perhaps it was still growling in its throat. His knees began to shake and he fell down. A few more toppled over him. And then with a sudden explosive boom, the stairs under his feet began to slide through the earth and sank into the netherworld.

He still was in the netherworld.

Bukhari had lost count of days. He had no idea how long he had been lying in this darkness, in this silence—a few days perhaps. Not a sound could be heard anywhere.

He tried to move his limbs but they seemed frozen, or rather, tied. A thought flashed through his mind: was he buried in his grave—the dirt, the cold stone and the darkness . . . had they buried him by mistake . . . or . . . or was he really dead? He tried to move his head, but simply couldn't. Perhaps he really was dead. And in a while Munkar and Naqir would be arriving, they would ask him to recite the *kalma*, reiterate his belief in the faith, in the creed. These two angels visit you on the third day after your death. That meant he had been dead for three days. It must be. If he was alive, he would have at least felt hungry. He felt strangely reassured that he was dead—he did not feel the pangs of hunger and yet his memory was all intact. He was not able to figure out whether he was lying face up or face down in the ground. He tried to remember the rites of burial—in which direction is the face when you are lowered into your grave? He began to feel sleepy again. There certainly was great comfort in death—an inebriation, a certain kind of intoxication.

The ground had begun to sway again. It was rocking, actually. And he was off to sleep—in his cradle. His grave was being rocked like a cradle. In a while, the angels would come—they would lift him in their arms and carry him away. He fell asleep.

His body felt light. He felt liberated from his physical body. There was no sensation in either his hands or his feet, or for that matter in any of his joints. His mind would occasionally flicker into life, glow dully for a while and then flicker off again. He now believed beyond doubt that he was lying in his grave and was dead. This is how things must be when one dies. And he began to wait for the arrival of the two angels. He felt a smile spread on his lips without making an effort to move them. A well-illuminated *ayat* crawled over his forehead and went past: *la ilaha illallah, Muhammadur rasulullah*—there is no god but Allah, and Muhammad is His messenger. His eyes were already closed but he pulled them shut once again. Once again he fell asleep. This time he did not wake for quite a few days. His own mind whispered to him, 'Now, I will get up on the day of *qayamat* only, on doomsday.'

His eyelids sprang open in one abrupt motion. His mind too sprung awake. Someone was lifting his eyelids and inspecting his eyes. He felt something crawling on his eyelids. And perhaps for the first time in days he felt air filling into his lungs. Perhaps people were making an effort to wake him up. Perhaps *qayamat* had finally arrived. He felt thin, scrawly lines squiggle on his eyelids, or were they somebody's fingers . . . or nails . . . or . . . or was it the whiplash of his mother's wet hair? Or was somebody writing something on his forehead with a razor-sharp nib?

Ayats, verses from the Quran, perhaps.

Somebody was scribbling something on the sole of one of his feet too. The right foot, or was it perhaps the left, he was not quite able to tell. Perhaps the angels were imprinting his good and bad deeds on the flesh of his body. He was smiling again without moving his lips. The bedlam of *qayamat* was coming nearer. He could make out the voices. And his eyes were now shutting, forever. The bulb flickered off, and he fell asleep. The grave once again began to rock. The angels had lifted him up and were carrying him away—down, further down. He was sinking more and more into the netherworld.

The rubble of buildings was finally being cleared. The earthquake had rumbled through them, ripping them apart, cracking them at the seams. As they cleared the rubble of the collapsed buildings they kept finding people—day after day—some injured, some wounded, some half-alive, some nearly dead and many long dead. They either cremated the dead bodies or buried them. Those that they could not immediately identify, they performed the last rites for later. The hospitals were bursting with the injured. Relief camps were opened at a number of places for the victims of the earthquake. Not only the government but common people were doing all they could do to help. Newspapers were organizing relief funds. In one of the newspapers that appealed to the public for donations, Bukhari's photograph was published.

After eighteen days under the earth, Bukhari had been rescued from the basement of Abbasi building. His entire body was crawling with cockroaches. But he was alive, albeit unconscious. His heartbeat was a little low but was still pulsating. He was immediately rushed to the hospital.

Bukhari woke up in the hospital a few days later and began to scream in pain. And he was heard shouting at the doctors, 'What sort of *qayamat* is this? What kind of hell have you people brought me into?'

Shortcut

The direct route was a long, winding road. Rising and falling, the road snooped around the hills and reached Banpur at its own leisurely pace. Then a straight run, all the way to Anandprayag in one single stretch. It was a proper pukka road but at places it came undone— with no traces of the tarred surface, just a cobbled bed of mud and stone chips. But that is how hilly roads are these days—they keep falling apart in the rains, and keep being rebuilt in the months of the dry sun.

We had stopped at a dhaba which turned out to be hardly a dhaba—it was more like a *dibba*, a small, boxed stall by the road, an excuse for a dhaba. There were three of us—Bhushan, Taran Taaran and me. We had stopped to have tea. We dipped our hands in the jar and took out some rusks and began to munch on them. Then we spotted some boiled eggs and were tempted to slice them, sprinkle some salt and pepper on them and gobble them up. But the eggs felt cold to the touch. We asked the shopkeeper to boil a dozen eggs afresh. We wanted to take them with us—the journey was quite long and the warm eggs would help us push swigs of brandy down our throats. It was disagreeably cold and we had bought a bottle of brandy on the way. When our breath got frozen during the ride we would unscrew the bottle, pour some into the cap and pour it down our throats. Our breath would thaw in the pipes for a while.

Getting the eggs boiled, munching on the rusks and chasing them down with cups of tea, we did not realize that we had ended up spending an hour and a half at that excuse of a dhaba. By now two trucks had pulled over and their drivers joined us at the dhaba. It had got pretty late and we realized that we would not reach Banpur before nightfall; and if the road ahead was anything like the one we had been travelling on so far, we wouldn't be reaching anywhere near Banpur before the middle of the night. Our driver told us about a shortcut to Banpur, about twenty or thirty kilometres down the road. The road wasn't in a great condition but it cut through the villages of Dheenu and Bamani, rose and fell along the river Alakananda and cut down the journey considerably. But in the same breath the driver advised us, 'What's the hurry, saab, to risk our lives now . . . our entire lives are left for that.'

Roads too stick out their tongues like a dog panting on its run. You can never tell when they are going to become thin, and when they will broaden. Unpaved roads are still easy to bear with. Paved, pukka roads are hair-raising. Every bend seems fatal. At every turn the mountain appears to be caving on to the road. And on top of it, the driver kept up his incessant chatter.

'When it caves in from above, the locals say the mountain has come.'

'And what if our ground gives in? If there's a landslide?' one of us asked.

He thought for a second and then said, 'The ones below us will say the mountain has come!'

'Or perhaps we may say that we have arrived.'

'We will hardly find the time to say anything, Bauji,' he laughed.

Every time he laughed, he would bounce on his seat, still holding onto the steering wheel.

Hilly roads have their own romance. We were driving in the sunshine when suddenly fog swooped down on the road, raising a curtain of fine, dense mist right in front of us and ordering us to halt—as if it was hiding a bathing beauty, trying to keep her away from our prying eyes. We kept waiting. The fog lifted in a while and, lo and behold, right before us stood a freshly bathed crescent of seven colours.

Hilly roads also tend to pick up pace as well as slacken sometimes—that's the reason why, on a slower patch of the road, you bump again into your co-traveller whom you had sped away from on a quicker one. At Devprayag, a car had sped past our jeep, honking: a small two-seater Herald. Our driver had quipped in Punjabi, 'Look at that, saab . . . the soap dish has sprouted wings'—and had once again started to bounce on his seat, laughing.

We had heard that a dam was going to be built at Devprayag and that the entire place would become submerged. It is at Devprayag that the Alakananda drains into the Ganga. We wanted to go and have a look. Taran Taaran said, 'If we are going that far, why not go a little further up and visit Rudraprayag too?' Bhushan suggested, 'In that case, let's go still further up, to Anandprayag. From there we can head off to Nainital via Dronagiri.'

We had been to Joshimath and Badrinath once before, the three of us.

We had hired the car from Delhi; by the time we reached Haridwar, it had begun to give trouble. The only place you could find a mechanic to fix your car was at the bus depot. At the depot we had bumped into the young *mahant* of Rishikesh ashram, Ashok Purohit. I knew him well. He had come to drop someone off in his car. Our driver had said, 'It's about an hour's job. Better to get the car fixed now . . . or else by the time we reach . . .' Ashok Mahantji had cut him off in mid-sentence and said, 'Go ahead . . . take your time . . . don't worry, I am taking them to Rishikesh in my car. When you reach Rishikesh, come straight to my ashram; you will find your sahibs there.' So from Haridwar to Rishikesh we had travelled in Ashok Mahantji's car.

Mahantji knew the perils of the hilly roads pretty well. He knew each and every turn of the serpentine road like the back of his hand. By the time our own car came to fetch us it was late at night. We spent the night at the ashram; and the next morning we got late leaving.

Mahantji sniffed the morning air and said, 'It seems it has snowed heavily at Joshimath.' We armoured ourselves in heavy-duty socks, gloves and mufflers and left.

It was now four hours since we had left the ashram. We had hardly started from the dhaba when the same Herald sneaked past us again.

The driver said, 'Saab, this soap dish of yours seems to be in some great hurry! Just doesn't give up!'

'Who's he?' we asked. 'The car seems to be from around here.'

'Yes, saab, it is!' he said. 'But the thing is, saab . . . you keep your old wife, but you must change your old car. This man seems to be glued to both. The day it squats down on the road, the in-laws will come to tow it away.'

He raised his rear from the seat; I braced myself against a dive into a pothole, but then he began to laugh. Bouncing away and laughing.

The drivers speak a different lingo—be they truckies or cabbies, their imageries are all linked to their vehicles. They are just too much in love with them. And quite often they substitute numbers for names.

'Oye *Chaunti-Chatti*, come on over . . . this side . . . take a swig . . . got some legs of chicken roasted.' This to the occupant of a vehicle with the license plate number 3436. I have overheard similar exchanges a number of times at dhabas.

When you begin your ascent into the mountains, you do feel as if you have left all your worldly cares below in the plains. Tall, majestic trees on either side of the road stand self-sufficient, the real claimants of the sky. If you walk in a jungle even for a little while, you are bound to find silences meandering about like Sufi mendicants, talking and listening in turn to their own selves.

The sun had slowly begun to slide down the distant hills. The sky, now with its kohl-black night-lined eyes, would peep through the hills time and again. After a while we saw the road which was the shortcut to Banpur. And in the distance we saw the very same Herald again. We tried to stop our driver, 'Veer Singh, why don't we too take this shortcut? If that old haggard Herald can, so can we—after all, we have a four-wheel drive.'

The driver stopped the jeep, mulled over the idea for a while and said, 'The Herald's his old nag, Sirji . . . and he doesn't have a load of passengers . . . but ours, if the road pushes her even a little . . .' He left the rest unsaid and retreated into silence. After a pregnant pause he added, 'Put a cushion under your bums . . . or else—' He began to bounce and laugh as he reversed the jeep and we were on the shortcut to Banpur.

What an enviable life the mountains lead! And their hilly roads! At some places the mountain walks by your side, leading you, holding your hand. At others, it picks you up like a fond father and props you up on its shoulder, and sometimes it puts you down to just watch you walk with unsure steps and keeps a watch on you from a distance. You keep on walking in your unsure steps, stumbling, reaching out for the hand of a river lest you fall . . . and you have no idea when the river lets go of you and you begin to walk on your own.

A petite waterfall suddenly came into view. We stopped our car and felt like soaking our tired feet in its pristine waters. But the biting cold was unrelenting and we were happy with just soaking the tires of our jeep in the water. We unscrewed the bottle of brandy and each of us poured a capful of brandy down our throats.

Suddenly the driver stopped the jeep and got down. We followed his gaze—an enormous boulder sat in the middle of the road along with a broken wheel and an axle. Veer Singh was peering down into the valley. When he did not move from his position for a long time, we too got off the jeep one by one. We hitched the legs of our trousers up to avoid the muddy slush and walked up to him. Deep down in the ravines we saw the Herald turned turtle, its top flattened against the rocky floor of the valley. And not far away from it we saw the driver, his body all askew. Veer Singh was looking for a way to climb down. Bhushan looked at him, affrighted, 'Any possibility that he may be alive?'

'Na ji!' he was choked with emotion when he spoke. 'The idiot, he took a shortcut there too.'

Pickpocket

Sultan was running towards the hospital. He had just got the news: his wife Zakia had gone into labour, her water had broken. She would give birth to the baby at any moment. The neighbour who had taken her to the hospital was the one who had told him.

'The doctors expected her to go into labour eight days later . . . but Bade Miyan, he . . .' Sultan nearly blasphemed. He bit his tongue, tugged at his own ears and slapped his own cheeks in quick repentance. He often called the Almighty Bade Miyan, the Big Man—more out of love and affection than anything else. It seemed to bring him closer to his maker.

When he heard the news, he had shot up from his seat and pulled his shirt over his head in such a great hurry that the seams had come a little more undone at the sides. He looked at the gaping hole at the armpit. Zakia often teased him, 'What have you left that hole for—to ventilate yourself? Come on, take it off, let me sew it up.'

But once he had put the shirt on, he felt too lazy to take it off. 'Oye, let it be, no problem . . . I will keep my arms stitched to my sides,' he would say. And then he would quip in an afterthought, 'But don't worry . . . when the little one comes I will get a new one stitched—I will then have to lift my arms to cradle him.'

Zakia would burst into laughter, 'Lo! You talk as if the baby's coming tomorrow or the day after . . . there's six more months to go . . . it's been only three months.'

'Three? This is the beginning of the fourth . . . why are you pushing it back further?'

His wife had conceived with great difficulty. They had pleaded with the Almighty, bowed their heads at numerous shrines. Their prayers were answered in the fourth year of their marriage. Six months seemed like years away to Sultan, and he broke down the months into weeks and the weeks into days—and counted the minutes and hours away.

He scrambled down the stairs and then remembered that he had left his wallet upstairs. He ran up the stairs again. He felt a little out of breath. He unlocked the door, walked in, and found the wallet where he had changed his shirt. It would have been pretty embarrassing to tell the doctor that he had forgotten his wallet at home. But Dr Chopra was a large-hearted man. He would have understood. He had been looking after Zakia's pregnancy ever since the conception.

'But the baby was to come eight days later. Now who hastened it up? Zakia? Or Bade Miyan?' he said to himself. He put his wallet in his pocket and headed back down the stairs. This time he negotiated one stair at a time. When he reached the ground floor he realized that he had forgotten to lock the door. And then he said to himself, 'No problem, Bade Miyan will look after the house.' He bit his tongue, tugged at his ears and slapped his cheeks.

Bade Miyan would look after the house—but what if he got late in reaching the hospital? By the time he scraped through the narrow lane to Rewari Bazaar, he was overwhelmed by the stench from the gutter. He reached the main road and started looking for an autorickshaw. A few of them careened off without stopping. A few were already occupied. Sultan was now becoming restless, panicky.

'Normally they keep scampering about in the traffic round the clock, but when you really need one, there is none!'

He picked up pace and began to run towards the hospital. But he kept turning his head in search of an autorickshaw—and kept bumping into dozens of pedestrians.

'Look where you are going!'

'Do your feet point backwards?'

Sultan knitted his brows at this turn of phrase. He was a collector of sorts of publicly expressed wisdom, but he hadn't heard this one before. A smile escaped his lips.

Suddenly he found an autorickshaw headed in his direction. When he waved his hand it swerved and sidled by his side as if it was his pet.

'Government hospital', he muttered, and got in. Had he just run he would have saved even these eight rupees—he had already covered half the distance. But when he slipped his hand into his pocket, it came through the other end. The wallet was missing; somebody had picked his pocket. He had not realized when. He put his hand over the rickshawallah's shoulder and showed him the picked seams of his pocket. 'Forgive me brother . . . somebody . . . on the way . . .' his voice got choked. The rickshawallah paused and then carried on, 'Not a problem . . . it happens sometimes.' He seemed to believe Sultan.

Sultan tried to remember when and where his pocket had got picked. And that was precisely what the rickshawallah asked him too, 'When did it happen? Where?'

'Right now! In the bazaar! I stay in Rewari Bazaar . . . just left the place . . . did not even realize when somebody— they stay unseen, friend, just like Bade Miyan, these pickpockets don't have a face . . . you never realize when they perform the sleight of hand.'

They reached the hospital. Sultan got off and wanted to tell the rickshawallah something but the man simply smiled and waved him off, took in another passenger and drove away.

Sultan's face fell. He entered the hospital with heavy steps and climbed the stairs to the second floor. He did not bother to take the lift. He stopped in front of Dr Chopra's chamber. There was a long line of people waiting. The orderly told him that Zakia had suddenly gone into labour and had been rushed into the operation theatre. Dr Chopra was still inside.

He found an empty bench outside the operation theatre and plonked down there. Time and again, his hand would slip into his picked pocket. And time and again the face of the rickshawallah would flash before him. Now he would have to narrate the entire pickpocketing incident to Dr Chopra too.

He did not realize when he had dozed off, how much time had passed. He woke up when Dr Chopra put his hand on his shoulder and took him inside his chamber.

'How's Zakia, Doctor sahib?'

'She's all right!'

'And the baby?' There was a smile on his face and a question in his eyes. 'Baby girl or baby boy?'

But when the doctor lowered his head, both his smile and his question were snuffed out.

'Sultan, the baby was stillborn.'

A chill ran down his spine. He kept looking at the doctor.

'Zakia's all right though. We had to sedate her . . . but she will be coming back into consciousness any time now.'

Sultan's eyes suddenly became dry. His hand slipped into his picked pocket. God alone knows why but he smiled. A little.

'What Bade Miyan! You turned out to be the biggest pickpocket of them all! You yourself blessed her womb, and then you yourself picked it! You pickpocket!'

VIII

A diamond may be cut by the petal of a flower
But even a chainsaw fails to cut through
The ties the umbilical cord binds—

Dusk

The fact that his missus had gone and got her long flowing tresses bobbed without so much as telling him irked Lalaji.

Last month, when their daughter-in-law went to visit her parents, she had taken the old woman along. The mother of a young infant on an arduous, long train journey needs all the help she can get. And it was not that Maya Devi had not consulted Lalaji. She had asked him, 'Bahu is asking me to accompany her to Delhi. Shall I?'

'Yes, certainly!' he had said. 'You should and you must! How is poor Bahu going to manage the kid all by herself in the train otherwise?'

Their daughter-in-law was named Mini. Her father was a colonel in the Indian Army—now retired. Both her brothers too were in the Army in high posts. Retirement had not affected the way Colonel sahib lived. His lifestyle remained the same. He still went to parties. His wife lived in style too. She was a modern woman—stylish to say the least. She had got her hair bobbed long ago; this time round she got Maya Devi's hair cut too.

When Maya Devi returned to Mumbai after her sojourn in Delhi, Lalaji was shocked to see her. Gone were her long flowing tresses.

'What have you done to your hair?'

'Mini's mother got them chopped.'

Maya Devi tried to laugh it off but when she caught the glimpse of brooding darkness swim across Lalaji's eyes, she could not help but shudder. She could read the tempest that brewed in the twin pools of his eyes. She had practiced the art of reading him to perfection over thirty-eight years of living together. A simper crawled out of her lips, trying to hide her embarrassment, 'It will grow back . . . in a matter of months.'

Lalaji did not utter a word. He quietly walked back into the house and plonked himself on the chair in the sitting room. He stayed in his cocoon at the dining table too—sat through his dinner enveloped in silence. Manoj tried to start a conversation but the wall was impenetrable. All he elicited from Lalaji was a nod or two. A worried Maya Devi asked, 'Are you feeling all right?'

His response had no bearing on her question. 'You had such beautiful hair . . . they looked so pretty. Why did you get them cut?'

When he did not get any response from Maya Devi, he added, 'And that too without even asking me!'

Manoj entered his room, scarcely able to contain his mirth. 'Babuji still worries about mother's braids. At his age! He must be touching what—seventy–seventy-two? And look at him, he is sulking like a teenaged lover.'

Mini, who was combing her elder daughter's hair, burst into laughter and asked, 'Was Babuji's a love marriage?'

'No! I was there at their marriage. Her parents forced the marriage on him.'

'How do you mean?'

'They had eloped and got married in court. About four–five years after their court marriage I was born. And only after my birth did their parents forgive them. There was a patch-up of sorts. Then when Ma and Babuji went to meet Ma's parents, they threw Babuji out of the house. They told him in no uncertain terms, only if he turned up formally at their door atop a wedding horse and with a wedding procession in tow would they think of giving him their daughter and grandson. That's when they got married—again. Not that I remember anything. But I know. We still have the wedding pictures.'

Lala Himraj always went out for a walk after dinner, every day without fail. It was an old habit of his. At the corner of the street was a paan shop where he would get his favourite condiments wrapped in a juicy betel-leaf. The betel nuts in his paan were getting fewer now, a kindness he showed to his ageing molars. But today he did not walk as far as the paan shop. He returned home much earlier, without his after-dinner paan. He just could not get over his wife's short hair. The image of his wife's barbered head eddied in his thoughts, pulling him deeper and deeper into a despondency from which he was unable to pull free. Was the sun setting on their love, were they at the dusk of their romance, hurtling towards a kind of darkness? Was it his right or his claim to demand that his wife conform to his vision? He could debate that endlessly; but the truth was that he felt as if he had been robbed of his most prized possession.

When Manoj was born he knew that he had to abdicate some of his claim over his wife. He had tried to laugh at his surrender, 'All right, all right! I will take out my own clothes. You look after your son. This pint-sized man has pushed me out of my own marital bed the moment he has been born.'

'Don't you go calling him pint-sized. A full eight pounds he weighs.'

'Fine, fine! But just tell me what I should wear! I have to meet Hilton sahib.'

'Just don't wear a necktie. It looks like a noose around your neck. A scarf is better.'

And then when Pinky was born there were further encroachments on his claim over his wife. The food laid on the table was now being cooked by a maidservant. But Maya Devi still seasoned the dal with her own hands. He would know if it wasn't done by her: Maya Devi took great pride in this fact. Then one day when Lalaji found a long black hair floating in his dal, he fired the maid. He told Maya Devi, 'If that hair was yours, I would have kept it in my wallet. But I will not tolerate this. If she wants to keep her job ask her to shave her head.'

'Arre hai! Shave her head? Why should she? Her husband's still alive!'

'Then hire a manservant.'

Ever since then, they had hired only manservants. And when the reins of the kitchen passed on to Bahu, Manoj's newly married wife, Lalaji told her, 'Don't let your hair loose when you are in the kitchen, Bahu. It gets in your eyes.' Mini immediately gathered her hair together in a tight bun. But the significance of Lalaji's words were not lost on Maya Devi. She knew that Lalaji could never forget that single hair floating in his dal all those years ago.

A few days passed in harmless banter. Maya Devi was thrilled in the furrows of her heart. She interpreted Lalaji's sulking as nothing but the signs of a robust love. But when a few more days passed, it began to sink in: Lalaji had stopped talking to her. Now she became totally restless, lovelorn. She found his sulking in his dotage more exacting, more punishing than their squabbles when they were young. The entire family would gather together at the dinner table. They began to eat their meals in oppressive silence. After dinner Lalaji would immediately go out for his walk; but now the walks were becoming shorter and shorter. When Maya Devi asked him why, he said, 'Now I tire pretty easily.'

A kind of desolation began to hang in the air, and along with it a sort of tension that was felt in the bones but never voiced—muted and yet there.

Once at the dinner table, Manoj said, 'Babuji, why don't you get yourself a new pair of spectacles? There are so many new designs available these days.'

'The ones that I am wearing were approved by your mother.'

'Ma chose this for you?' Mini looked a little surprised.

'Yes! She did not like the round frames so I began to wear these rectangle-shaped ones. And then when she objected to the black frames I bought the brown ones.'

At the dinner table another day, he suddenly shot a glance at Maya Devi and asked, 'Did you season the dal yourself today?'

Maya Devi looked at him with a tenderness that welled up in her eyes. She was touched that he could still discern her touch.

Mini asked, 'How did you know?'

'Bahu, I can smell your mother-in-law's hands in the dal's seasoning.'

But the silence remained unbroken. And when all indirect efforts to placate Lalaji failed, Mini broke down before him and offered her unconditional apologies. 'Forgive me, Babuji, it was my mistake. I should have stopped Mummy. I should have been more firm with her when she took Mummy to the parlour. I couldn't say no to Mummy, but Mummy also agreed.' Mini called them both Mummy, her mother as well as her mother-in-law.

'The world does not come to an end when somebody gets their hair shorn,' Lalaji said with a muted smile. 'It's a small little thing. But then it is always the small little things that season life . . . the things that make life worth living. She and I have become old . . . but have we also become strangers to each other now?'

The next day, Lalaji announced, 'I am going to visit Pinky. I will stay with her for a few days. I need a change of air.'

Pinky lived in Jabalpur. After a little deliberation they all agreed. Manoj even tried to joke, 'Yes, that's good . . . by the time you are back I am sure Ma's hair will have grown a bit longer.'

Maya Devi said, 'Come back soon. It is not considered good to stay long at one's daughter's.'

Lalaji left the following day.

A few days passed, and then a few more. A week went by. Lalaji had failed to arrive at Pinky's. Everyone began to worry. They began to look for him at his friends', at his relatives'. What if he had met with some accident? But if that was the case, then they would have been informed, wouldn't they? They could not think of any plausible reason for his disappearance. When their search and queries did not return any results, they informed the police, published his photograph in newspapers. But there was no trace of Lalaji. Now they began to imagine the worst. All kinds of thoughts began to criss-cross through their minds.

Two and a half months passed. And then they got a letter—from an ashram in Badrinath. Lala Himraj was terribly ill. His condition was deteriorating every day. A pundit from the ashram had found their address from his diary and written to them.

They immediately left for Badrinath. But when they reached, they found that they were a bit too late. Lala Badrinath had passed away that very morning. He now had a beard, overgrown, unkempt. His ungroomed, uncut hair was matted. Lying on the mat, he looked like a sanyasi.

Maya Devi broke every single one of the bangles that adorned her wrists. Then she walked up to him and whispered into his ears, 'Shall I cut my hair? Now I have to get it completely shorn. I am a widow after all.'

And this time round, she cut her hair with her husband's permission.

Dadaji

Dadaji sauntered towards the settee, tapping across the courtyard with his walking stick, and sank into it.

Pulling Jaswant's son down from the tree and thrashing him was the cause of Dadaji's grief. And you could hardly call it a thrashing—a few slaps on his buttocks, a scolding, that was all.

Since Bunty had come to the village, he was always up to something—he was always pulling a prank, or picking a fight. He just couldn't keep still. Just the other day, he was skipping stones across the pond with that village kid, Beru. Now he could not have learnt this in the city. The stones can only skip in a village pond, you can't make them skip on the waters of the sea. To pick up a light, flat stone—or a broken pot rim ground into a round flat shape—and throw it across the pond so that it bounces off the surface of the water 3–4 times before sinking, is an art. Beru proudly proclaimed that he could make the stone bounce at least five times before it sank, sometimes six, even seven. Bunty had a brainwave; he broke some porcelain plates and brought the shards to contest with Beru. Because they were so smooth, he thought they would skip far across the pond.

Beru was the washerman's son. He would come every day to the house to pick up laundry. He was the one who helped Dadaji solve the mystery of the broken plates. Dadaji tried to drill a lesson into Bunty, 'Son, you don't break your china for a skipping-stones game!' It was not difficult for Bunty to guess the name of his betrayer. He pushed Beru into the lake. Beru was a village kid—he swam right back to the shore. But Bunty hadn't learnt to swim—he couldn't even paddle in shallow water. In the fracas he had fallen in the water himself; he barely managed to keep himself afloat, and somehow managed to avoid drowning.

But Bunty was angry at Dadaji over this morning's thrashing.

Nobody these days stayed in touch through letters. Jaswant had installed a phone for his father's use. Bunty rang up his father and asked him to come and pick him up immediately. He had had enough of the village. He would rather spend the rest of the holidays in the city itself.

Dadaji was worried, and a little heartbroken too. It is true that when you have children of your own, your attachment with your parents grows a little less. You become more attached to your kids. Jaswant would certainly not be able to remember the time when he had wanted to step out barefoot in the rain and had got scolded, 'Go! Wear your boots first!' Mother couldn't bear to see Jaswant being yelled at. She would scoop him up in her arms and run out.

Anything could have happened . . . How was he to tell Jaswant that his younger sister had run barefoot in the rain and had been stricken with polio? Her right leg had just dried up. Dadaji had witnessed how difficult it was for his parents to marry his polio-stricken sister off. Over the years Dadaji had collected so many memories that every incident would unravel yet another story. Now if you did not share your experiences, if you did not talk about them, then what were they for? Wasn't this what growing old and wise was all about?

It was his growing old that Jaswant was worried about. When he had retired from the Bank of Baroda, he had thought of the old family house in the village. Jaswant was the one who had said that they had kept going to the old house when he was in school, to visit his grandfather. But now, nobody lived in the house.

'Why don't you go and have a look at it?' Jaswant had said. 'Do whatever you deem fit—renovate it, sell it, whatever. Anyway it will not be easy for you to live on your pension in the city. And now that Bunty has started school, the expenditures are mounting.'

Dadaji had understood what his son had left unsaid. But he had grown pretty attached to Bunty. Since the time his wife had died he had been spending more and more time with his grandson. Grandfather and grandson made an excellent pair of raconteurs—they would regale each other with their stories; Bunty would tell his tales of cricket and Dadaji would talk of his adventures with gilli-danda.

When Jaswant's wife became pregnant for the second time, Dadaji had left for the village. His heart had sort of wilted. But once he was in the village, it sprouted new greens, as if a plant plucked out of the earth had struck new roots. The floodgates of memories opened. He began to think about his own days with his grandfather. If truth be told, the love and affection he had got from his elders while growing up, his own children could never get. His father used to walk four kos to the madrasa. He himself used to cycle to high school. And even when he had begun to stay in the college hostel, every month his grandfather would arrive with a fresh supply of home-made ghee and pinni. This old house had been built by his grandfather. He had seen the house grow—some room or veranda constantly being added to it, by his grandfather, by his father. The concrete roof was laid while he was in college. It was in the newly built barsati that he had puffed his first cigarette and it was there that he had been caught. It was on that very roof that he had been caned, with a supple branch freshly snapped off the tamarind tree. It was on the roof that he had fallen in love. And it was the drainpipe off the roof that he had climbed down to elope.

Jaswant had not even needed to run away. One fine day, when he fell in love, he just walked into the house with the girl, introduced her to his mother and simply declared his love for her and his intention to marry her. That was all. Yes, he did get yelled at. But Dadaji could not remember ever raising his hand on Jaswant. Then . . . how come he had thrashed Bunty today?

With Jaswant's arrival, Bunty grew more distant. He stopped talking to Dadaji altogether. Jaswant tried to instil some sense into him, but Bunty was adamant. In the morning when they were leaving, Jaswant told Bunty, 'Go touch Dadaji's feet.' Bunty turned his face away.

Dadaji walked up to him and ruffled his hair. Tears welled up in his eyes.

'So, you are not going to talk to me, eh?'

'No. Never!'

'Why?'

'Why did you pull me down from the tree and hit me?'

'It wasn't you I hit, son. I hit someone else.'

Bunty looked at Dadaji through tear-filled eyes.

'Yes, son . . . I hit that boy who had fallen from the tree a long time ago and broken his leg. Look here . . .'

And Dadaji sat down on the settee and pulled his trouser-leg up and showed Bunty the scar on his shin.

'See! I was your age then. And look at me . . . how I limp to this very day.'

And limping, he walked his son and grandson to the waiting taxi.

The Adjustment

It was a mistake not to take Nana, our grandfather, to the funeral of our grandmother, our Nani.

A few months ago, Nana had suffered a stroke. We were scared for his health and did not want him to be exposed to further trauma. He had lived with Nani for over half a century, seen her radiant face every day of those years. Must he see her face in death? Must he see her put atop a funeral pyre and set afire? He too agreed, 'Go, take her away . . . whisper into her ears that I too am on the way, not far behind; tell her I will see her in the beyond.'

With heavy hearts we hoisted Nani's bier over our shoulders. I turned to look, just once, and found Nana stepping away from the balcony into the room, pulling the door shut after him.

Nani was about three years younger than Nana and she passed away three years before he did. Nana was

212

very old and weak at the time Nani died. He must have been what, about eighty-five, and yet he would find something to cavil at everything Nani did. He would keep quibbling with her, as if they were two people who had just married in the first flush of love and were still discovering each other. At times a spat spiralling out of hand would push them into silence. They would stop talking to each other for days together. When we would try to intervene, all Nana would do was quip, 'It happens son, it happens . . . it takes time to adjust to each other.'

How much longer would he need to adjust? He must have been not more than twenty-five when they got married. He had now spent nearly sixty years with her. 'How do you think it went?' he would say. 'The first twenty years, she stayed sterile. And then when she became fertile, she gave me a daughter and chopped away her womb.'

It was fun listening to him talk. Mother would always reprimand us, 'You people provoke him and my mother has to bear the brunt.' Her mother, meaning our Nani. And Nani would whoosh out a few words together from her toothless mouth, 'Be grateful that I gave you two grandsons . . . now for the love of God, just shut up!'

Nana would shut up, but would manage to somehow say something with his eyes in a language that only Nani could understand, scalding, scorching her to her core. We could only make a feeble attempt to hear the unspoken words through the occasional deep-seated sighs that escaped Nani's lips.

My brother and I were at a very young, impressionable age when our father married a second time. He would often strut into the house with his new wife. Mother was helpless. There was nothing she could do about it, but Nani fought with her, and scooped the two of us into her arms and brought us into her house, saying, 'You want to rot here, do so . . . but I am not letting my grandchildren stay here to get thrashed by their stepmother.'

Perhaps this did not make Nana happy.

'Couldn't birth sons herself and now she has gone and brought over somebody else's . . . who's going to raise them?'

A few years down the line when our stepmother became pregnant, Mother too came over to Nana's for good. Nana got further irritated. He would turn his face away whenever he saw Mother. Nani did her best to make him understand. But he stayed put, adamant in his thinking. If there was something to be done, his opinion to be sought, it was us two brothers who would go to him as Mother's emissary. If anyone got her way with Nana, it was Nani. She would tell it to his face, 'You will regret it the day I die. You don't speak with the mother of these two children. They are also not going to talk to you. You will sit all by yourself in the balcony and bathe in the sun and your own loneliness.'

Nana would say, barely audibly, 'I am older than you. You just wait and watch who's going to go first, you or I?'

Nani would neither cluck her tongue nor touch her ears, like other old women do to shoo the mention of death away. She would simply say, 'Yes, you will see. Just watch!'

And Nani really did leave before him. Nana became all the more irritable now—as if he had lost a wager. For a few days he took out his anger on his food. He would push away his plate and say, 'Tell her I don't want to eat!'

He imprisoned himself in the bedroom. We removed a few of Nani's belongings to make the room liveable for Nana but he did not let us cart away Nani's bedstead. In a dry, hollow rasp, he said, 'Let it be . . . where else is she going to sleep?'

The day we had to take Nani's ashes away for immersion, that day too Nana stayed locked in the room. When I went in, I found him sitting on her bed. He just touched the urn and said, 'Take him away . . . all my life he just kept fighting with me.'

The shift was gradual. I did not pay much heed to it that first day but later it became more evident.

Another day I caught him taking Nani's cough syrup. He was measuring it by the capful, exactly the way Nani used to. I asked him, 'What's that you are doing?'

'What am I supposed to do then . . . this darned cough just doesn't let up!'

Exactly the same turn of phrase that Nani would have used.

He paused, threw me a look and said, 'When this bottle gets over, get me a new one.'

I was a little taken aback. I had never heard him coughing. But this was nothing compared to the shock he gave me a few days later.

I told him, 'Nana, let's go to a salon. You need a haircut.'

Nana looked at me, scandalized by the idea.

I insisted, 'If you don't want to go, then I will call a barber over.'

He did not even deign to look at me this time. He began to shake his head, 'No, no, he will kill me. He does not like my hair cut short . . . he will never approve!'

His intonation was nasal, exactly like Nani's. It seemed as if it was Nani who was speaking. I moved back, a little worried. When I told Mother about it, she said, 'These days he's begun to miss Mother too much. I have seen him talking to her photograph. He has even begun to sleep in her bed.'

But Mother was startled the day she prepared Nana's favourite raita and he returned it without even touching it, saying, 'Don't you know that I don't like raita in the night? It makes my throat sore.'

His entire constitution had begun to morph. He had increasingly begun to talk in a feminine way. I was beginning to get worried about him. I had a friend, Dr K.D. Kamble, a psychiatrist. I called him over.

He talked to Nana at length—for hours. Most of the time, Nana kept quiet. He did not answer most of Dr Kamble's queries. But when he did, he spoke like Nana normally did and in his own voice. Something else became evident too: to one of the numerous questions that Dr Kamble asked him, he said, 'This only she can answer. I will ask her when she comes.'

Dr Kamble shot back, 'Where has she gone?'

The ends of his lips curled up a little in a smile, 'Oh . . . she doesn't really ever tell me her whereabouts.'

When Nana left, Dr Kamble said, 'He does not perceive your Nani as dead. He has begun to live a double life. In fact there's more of her and less of him. He has begun to think of himself as Nani. Whatever happens, it happens to her. She is the one who needs to be fed. She is the one who feels thirsty. She is the one who feels the pain. And it is she who takes the medicines. He only swallows the pills on her behalf.'

I drove the good doctor back to his home. He said that Nana was suffering from a sort of dissociative personality disorder. The condition was little understood, he said, and there was no sure cure for it. He said, 'We will keep at it, do our best. Sometimes, in certain cases, there is some improvement; in some cases, everything returns to normal, without our even doing anything. But at your Nana's age, that kind of recovery is nearly impossible.'

Dr Kamble invited me in, and fortified my frayed nerves by pouring me a stiff peg of whiskey. We talked for a while, a little of this, a little of that; as I was about to leave, he asked me, 'Tell me one thing—how does it make any difference to you whether he is Nana or thinks himself to be Nani? How does it change anything whether he eats raita by staying your Nana, or refuses to eat raita by morphing into your Nani? I am not saying that it does not sound a bit strange and a bit awkward—but let him be. Let him live his life any way he wants to.'

I was late coming back home, but I did feel quite unburdened by what Dr Kamble had said, a lot

less worried. I thought the way Nana had made his
adjustments with Nani, we too should make our
adjustments with him.

When I reached home, I found that Rachna had not yet
eaten. When I asked her she said, 'Even Nana has gone
off to sleep without eating anything. Go and ask him at
least. I don't want him to have to wake us when he gets
up in the night, hungry.'

When I walked into Nana's room to wake him up, I
found him sleeping in Nani's bed. I lifted the blanket to
wake him up. I was stunned. He was sleeping in Nani's
dhoti and blouse.